PROLOGUE

January 1, 2021, Falls Church, Virginia

TRUMAN MITCHELL, known by everybody as 'Mitch' drove the white van in the holiday traffic north on I-95 toward Washington D.C. If there was ever a good time to be traversing the Beltway traffic, this would probably be it. That would be in a normal year. This was not to be a *normal year*, in any sense of the term.

Two major events would guarantee that political staffers, and probably the elected officials themselves would be back on the job well before when they normally would have. If everything went according to plan our next President would be sworn in on January 20th. In addition to that, and some would say more importantly, there would be a critically important run-off election in Georgia.

On January 5th Georgia voters would decide the futures of two senatorial seats in a run-off election. For a margin of safety, the Republicans hoped to win both seats. It was critically important, however that they win *one* seat. This would keep the Democrats from having the all-important tie-breaker vote of the Vice President. If the Dems should win both seats, their party would have a strangle hold on any votes in either house that followed the party line. They would effectively control all three branches of government.

As Mitch drove, he let his mind wander a bit. His chest could swell with pride that he held sway over a lot of what had happened in the political arena of late. He was an uneducated man, 56 years of age, and he had done well for himself.

Mitch grew up in the streets of Detroit. He did not know who his father was, and his mother could not control her desire for drugs and alcohol. Mitch had an older brother who took him under a protective wing when he was only fourteen. The brother was two years older but had the street-wisdom of much older men. His brother was bigger and stronger than Mitch and was protective of his younger sibling. So it was that Mitch learned how to survive in the streets. He dropped out of school at the end of his sophomore year and started to support himself.

Having the bigger, stronger brother helped Mitch at first. It was 'survival of the fittest' and Mitch needed protection. He was not a big man. As such he was often picked on and intimidated. What Mitch had in abundance was common sense. He knew that he would not always have his brother's protection, and he learned how to survive using his wits.

Mitch's brother died at age 21 as the result of gang violence. For about a year before that happened, the brothers' roles were reversed. That is not to say that Mitch was a physical threat, or that people didn't try to intimidate him. That part didn't change. Mitch matured in other ways, however. He found that most of the people he dealt with were lacking in brain power. He tried to help his brother make his way, but somehow his overtures were rejected.

On the day after his brother's funeral, Mitch took stock of his life and how it would be for him to be totally on his own. The one lasting change that had occurred was when he was introduced to 'The Boss.' That was the beginning of an apprenticeship for Mitch in the gang. He had the ability to fill the mental gap that often arose in gang activities. More than once he was the one who figured out solutions to problems when they happened.

The Boss was a man named Wade Dilmore. He had risen to the top of the local crime organizations due to his own hard work and dedication. This had not been easy. The 'muscle' was readily available in his underlings, but the 'smarts' was in short supply. He soon recognized that Mitch had the ability to provide a buffer zone for him in his dealings with the street people. If the gang had been a legitimate organization, the Boss elevated to the CEO function and Mitch became the General Manager.

Riding with Mitch that day were two of his loyal companions. Robert Ball, 'Bolo' had been a lifelong friend and was now, due to his physical stature, often Mitch's protector. He could handle himself in a fight and was ready to do so when needed. He was a bulky six-footer and was strong as a bull. Arnold Dinsmore, 'Dinny' was the type of man that offered blind obedience. He was not one who could think for himself and often got into trouble if he tried to. He required a closer degree of supervision but his performance within his range of abilities was acceptable. Dinny was a lanky six foot three and skinny as a rail. Both Bolo and Dinny had been with Mitch for years.

"How much longer?" asked Dinny. He had the patience of a six-year-old.

"The traffic is worse than I expected," said Mitch. "I'm guessing it will be another hour."

They were headed for Falls Church, Virginia. Mitch had punched in the address of the hotel that was their destination. Thank goodness for the GPS. When they got onto the

Beltway, driving was a real challenge. One had to be careful to be in the proper lane for navigating in the heavy traffic. Mitch had Bolo help him watch for exit lanes. His usual method of driving in heavy traffic was to stay in the right-hand lane. This didn't work well on the Beltway due to the high speed of the traffic. It was easy to be trapped in that lane and be forced off an exit you didn't want to take.

"I should have had Bolo drive," thought Mitch. "It would have been worth listening to his cussing at the other drivers." He made a mental note to put Bolo behind the wheel after their next stop.

They got off the Beltway and headed toward their hotel. It was only a short distance, and the traffic was more reasonable. The Boss had told Mitch a little of what to expect. Even with that knowledge, he was blown away when he saw the place. This was a first-class joint. They were accustomed to staying at the medium-priced chain motels when they travelled. This was above and beyond. It was owned by one of the Boss's business associates. According to what Mitch was told, the man owned several hotels in this category in some major metropolitan locations around the country. Mitch's business head told him that this was probably a sophisticated money-laundering operation, one that far surpassed anything they had seen in the Boss's territory.

When they checked in, they were given separate rooms, and were told they could use their room key card to charge meals and bar expenses. In addition to that they could tell the concierge if they would like to have any 'female company' in their rooms during their stay.

This was to be an extended weekend R & R vacation for the gang. They had performed well in several events during the past year. Their last gig was in Atlanta. Before that they were in Pittsburgh, Philadelphia, Portland, Seattle, and Denver. In Detroit, their home turf, they took the leading role.

The Boss's group handled the events in Detroit and coordinated with the outside players from other groups. His own gang handled 'elections', 'ballots', 'drop-boxes', bribes, and other menial functions that helped achieve their local and statewide goals. The duties were compartmentalized so that secrecy could be maintained in the overall grand plan. At times they needed the help of poll workers and union officials to succeed in their efforts. In these cases, they dealt only with the top people directly. The rank and file didn't have a clue.

Mitch was able to extrapolate what he knew of the local operation into what he perceived to be the grand plan for the entire country, or at least portions thereof.

The payoff was achieved back in November. The balance of the electoral college tallies fell in favor of the Democrats. The entire nation was stunned. How could this have happened? Only a few people knew the answer to that. Mitch knew.

CHAPTER 1

Mitch's phone rang at 7 A.M. It took him a minute to realize where he was as he rolled out of bed to answer it. It was his cell phone. Who could be calling him at this hour? He was instantly awake when he heard the Boss's voice.

"Hello," said Mitch. "What's up?" He was surprised that the Boss was calling him. He had just reported in when they arrived at the hotel the evening before.

"Change of plans, Mitch. I won't be able to attend the meeting. Something's come up that I can't get out of. I need you to go in my place," said the Boss. "I've already contacted the chairman of my group and made arrangements for you to fill in for me. He wasn't too happy with the substitution, but this is too important to not have our part of the plan represented. I can't talk about it on the phone, but I'm counting on you to handle the details of our part. You haven't met any of these men. They are my top-level business associates. I'm counting on you to do this for me. Most of the plan has been worked out, but this meeting is necessary to flesh out the details. The Secretary will give you a copy of the minutes of the meeting when you leave. Make sure you protect it at all costs. Be at meeting room A at nine AM. Ask for the Chairman. Any questions?"

"Can I contact you if there are any problems?"

"Only in an emergency, and in that case send me a text. You make the decisions Mitch. Make this work. It could be a step to a higher level for you in the future. Phone me when you get back before you get to the warehouse."

When they disconnected Mitch took a deep breath and sat down on the bed. This was a big surprise for him. For all these many years he had been a loyal soldier in the organization, never expecting to have an opportunity like this. It was like getting a tryout for the major leagues. He had less than two hours to get his act together before the meeting.

The first thing he did was to leave messages for Bolo and Dinny. There was no use trying to phone them. They were probably sleeping off bad hangovers after the amount of free liquor they had consumed last night. He told them they were on their own today and to meet him for dinner. He would call later to tell them what time. They were told not to call him, that his phone would be turned off.

Mitch didn't have a clue as to how he should dress for the meeting. He decided to wear the sports coat he had in his luggage and to carry a tie with him. He would hang back to try and get a look at the others before he went in. The necktie would be knotted and in his coat pocket. He could step around a corner and slip it over his head if necessary. When he was ready, he went down to have some breakfast. He needed to settle the butterflies in his stomach.

In the dining room he took notice of three other men. Each was eating alone, and each was wearing a tie. He went into the men's room and put his on. When he got to the meeting room, he hung back a little. Men were entering without knocking, so that's what he did.

Inside was a banquet table with rows of ID labels. The man behind the table wore a label that said 'Secretary.' Mitch went up to him and introduced himself. The Secretary told him they didn't use names in the meeting. He picked up a name tag for Mitch that had the alpha/numeric code 'M2' on it.

"I was told to ask for the Chairman," said Mitch.

"Take a seat for now," said the Secretary. "He will get the meeting started and then introduce you to the rest of the group. See me after the meeting to pick up your copy of the minutes. Leave your phone on the table. You can pick it up on your way out."

Mitch sat in an empty chair near the front. He counted ten men in the room so far, and there were still two more empty seats. They were mostly quiet, but he noticed a couple of whispered conversations near the back. Apparently at least a few of them knew each other. He occupied himself with trying to figure out the code on the name tags. The capital letter could stand for a state, or possibly a city. Most of the numbers were either a 1 or a 2. He saw one number 3. While he was still contemplating this, the other two men came in. In addition to them, an impressive looking older man in an expensive suit came up and got the badge that said 'Chairman.'

The room was wired for sound. The Chairman didn't waste any time with pleasantries. After shaking hands with the Secretary, he went directly to the microphone.

"Welcome everyone. I'm glad you could make it. Before we get into the details of this special meeting, let me introduce a first-time representative to the group. Mr. M2 please stand," he said.

After he stood and the group had a look at him, Mitch sat down. The Chairman continued. "I am going to go over a couple of the basic ground rules for the benefit of M2. As you are aware, we do not use names, but rather this code to identify ourselves. Many of you will know each other professionally, but while you are here, please use the code rather than names. This also goes, especially for any time you might meet during one of our planned jobs. This is for the protection of all of us. In the event you run afoul of the law, clam up. We have the best lawyers that money can buy. The best outcome for you will be to rely on them. Do not discuss the critical aspects of this job outside of this room. There are cameras and ears everywhere. Do not discuss anything with your underlings that they do not 'need to know'. Be careful about telephone conversations, both cell and landline. Neither are secure. Vet your employees and your subcontractors. This mission is too important to have it screwed up because of our own sloppy practices. Know that you can trust everyone in this mission. Now let's get on with the program for today. We have a short slide presentation for you about our objective, the U. S. Capitol."

CHAPTER 2

Mitch watched attentively as the slides showed pictures of the Capitol, both outside and inside. There were detailed photos of the various security measures that were employed in and around the building. He was amazed at how easy it must have been to get this information. Many of the cities where they had 'protested' had security measures superior to these. Any tourist could have taken these pictures.

The Chairman gave a running narration with the slide show. He explained that this was only an overview, and that the detailed assignments would be divided among those present at this meeting. The slide presentation was followed by a 'question and answer' period.

After the questions had slowed down, the Chairman spoke again. "I want to give you a few 'mission specific' rules," he said. "We don't know how many people will be attending the Trump rally. We suspect the number will be in the hundreds of thousands. We plan to time our movement on the Capitol to blend in with the crowd movement. Think of it as riding a surfboard. If all goes well, we should be able to ride the wave right into the building. We have all seen the Trump rallies on TV. His crowds always have people who get fired up about what he has to say. We expect a lot of them to be in DC that day. We are calling them 'volunteers.' They will help provide the wave for us to ride to our objective. They are our unpaid helpers."

"That brings me to the specific rules involving the volunteers. Do not get into any altercations with them. Try to think of them as allies. If we keep a low profile, they will get the attention of the security cameras and law enforcement. A lot of them will be recognized with the facial recognition capabilities that are sure to be employed. We want the follow-up effort to end in dead-end trails when the law goes after them. They love to get on Facebook. We don't want to. We don't want any of our people to be 'carrying', either guns or knives. There will probably be a couple of right-wing groups present with their costumes and their flags. We may have a little of that, but it will be controlled. Let them take the heat."

"Now, about the Capitol police. Again, the volunteers will make up much of the push needed to overcome them. We will have a formidable force with our own people, but ours will have specific assignments to deal with. Our people will be the impetus for breaching the exterior and interior chamber doors. Again, the volunteers will help. Our people will scale the exterior walls to gain access to the balconies. Who knows? There may even be some volunteers capable of doing this as well. Once on the balconies, we will smash out the windows to access the interior hallways. Our information is that the Capitol police force is not adequate to stop us. Don't be surprised if you see someone in a police uniform ease the way for us. They may or may not be ours. This mission should be a lot easier than some we have had in the major cities."

"Once we are inside, we attend to our own objectives. Let our friends, the volunteers smash, take selfies and grab souvenirs. If we see a loose laptop or cell phone, grab that. It could have valuable intelligence. It would be a good idea to have one of your crew members wear a small backpack to get that out through the crowd."

"Some of you are not staying at this hotel. We have street maps for each of you. We suggest that you have transportation for your crew located within walking distance of the objective. Predetermine your walking route to the transport as well as your driving route out of the city or to your hotel. Traffic will be bad with all those people trying to get somewhere else. Have your assigned driver memorize the route and destroy the map. Do a practice run on Tuesday at rush hour. Do another run on Tuesday evening, if you need to work out any glitches."

"This will be the most important mission we have had since this all started. Blame is the name of the game. The Republicans blame the Democrats because most of the 'smash and grab' operations have been in Democratic run cities. The Democrats blame the Republicans, mostly Trump, for not sending in the troops to quell the riots. If we are successful, most likely Trump will be blamed. The Democrats will make political points for use in their impeachment proceedings. You can be sure that the news media will be all over this."

"The news spotlight will be on everybody who gets within spitting distance of the Capitol. We need to use any means possible to have the volunteers take the heat for us. Deflect that attention until we are well clear of the city. That means being tight-lipped after the event, especially at your hotel or in the public in general. Cover anything that could be seen through a car window that might incriminate you. Don't wear any of your MAGA gear after you get out of the Wednesday crowd. Get a duffel bag to stash it in and put it into your trunk out of sight. Don't try to get rid of it until you get well out of the D.C. area. You could be seen and photographed. In today's world you could wind up being a movie star on the internet."

"Gentlemen, this mission carries with it more *risk* than any of our previous ventures. There are many ways we are exposed, and it will take our combined best efforts to succeed. If we win, we win big. If we fail, the fallout could extend into our own local organizations. We cannot let that happen. Govern yourselves accordingly. Now, we are going to break for lunch. We will reconvene here at 1 PM and break into groups where we will plan specific objectives. Enjoy your lunch."

"Mr. M2, I need a minute with you before you go to lunch."

Mitch stayed in the room until everyone except the Chairman and the Secretary had left.

"I was not happy about the eleventh-hour substitution of your organization's representative," said the Chairman. "I'm sure you can see by now why I feel that way. However, it would be foolish of me to change our plans for the division of labor at this late date. Your Boss has a great deal of respect for your ability to fill in for him, so we are keeping with the plan. You will be handling the responsibilities of M2 in addition to your own participation on the ground. Don't let us down."

"Thank you, Chairman," said Mitch. "You can count on me."

The Chairman handed Mitch a business card. On the card was printed, simply 'Chairman', followed by a phone number.

"That number is for a 'burner-phone'. If you run into a problem, you can reach me for help. When the mission is complete, the number will no longer exist. Each of the men in this room have this card. One more thing. You will be coming back here for one more night when the mission is complete. Before you head for home the following morning, you will be given a package to take with you. This will be the cash payment for the M2 part of a successful job.

You may need some of that for expenses in getting home. We would prefer that you not use credit cards for anything on the trip. In case you are wondering, this mission is being financed by Mr. $. That's the way we refer to him, and that's all you need to know about him. I'll see you after lunch."

CHAPTER 3

When Mitch got back from lunch, there were several conversations going on in the room. The Chairman had not yet returned, and the atmosphere had loosened up to a degree. He noticed that Mr. N1 had a definite New York accent. There was also no mistaking Mr. G1 and his southern accent. He was no doubt from Atlanta.

Mitch's thoughts were interrupted by the return of the Chairman. He wasted no time in getting the larger body divided into smaller groups. Mitch found himself in a group with Mr. M1 and Mr. M3. Again, based on their accents, he pegged M1 as Minnesota and M3 as Maryland, (Minneapolis and Baltimore). He was starting to figure it out. The degree of sophistication of the code was not as important as the adherence to its principals.

Before they could get started with their group planning, the Secretary handed Mitch a card that said, 'Wild Card'. "What's this?" asked Mitch.

"This indicates that you will have subcontractors under your command," said the Secretary. "In this case there will be three additional men working with you. They will arrive here on Monday, in time to train with your regular people. They are former Russian circus performers. All speak English with little or no accent. Their names are on the back of the card. We use only the first name, again for security purposes.

"Tats" is a former 'strong-man'. He will join with M2's group in breaching the doors. M1 and M3 will each provide one man for that effort, under the command of M2."

"Bones and Oreo are former acrobats. They will work with others, jointly provided by M1 and M3, and will be under their joint command. They will be scaling the exterior walls and entering the building from the balconies. When the mission is complete, the three Wild Cards will combine with the M2 crew and meet here at this hotel. They will leave here together and will travel to the home territory of M2 where they will report for future duty. M2 will cover their expenses for the trip. Is that all clear to each of you?"

"Do they understand who will be in charge, both for the mission and later for the trip?" asked Mitch.

"They understand, and they come highly recommended. But if there is a problem, call the Chairman. He will deal with it."

Mitch found both his counterparts to be helpful and intelligent. Once they worked through the details of their own responsibilities, they moved to a discussion of how their parts fitted into the plan.

"I have some concerns about our ability to move forward through the crowds," said Mitch. "We have no idea how many people will be in attendance."

"Follow your big men through," said Mr. M-1. "Have them open a passage using a swimming motion with their elbows and shoulders. A polite 'excuse please' will help but follow it up with immediate forward movement. The next man should follow on the heels of the leader so nobody can stop your flow. Some of the volunteers will want to move with you, and that's okay. They are especially helpful when you get to the police crowd-control barriers. Your people need to be like football linemen with their blocking sleds. Your side will have the advantage because you will have your big guys in front. Their line will be haphazard. They don't know how to plant themselves to stop the flow. At a point, it will be to your advantage to lift the barricade. This will allow your people to get under and past. Then, just push it aside."

"Sometimes the police will use shields and their batons," said Mr. M-3. "When they hold the sticks horizontally you can force their arm upwards, above the head, and throw their balance off enough so they can't swing the thing. This will turn the man, shield and all, and allow your smaller men to slip through their line. Once through, you can break up their line with a foot behind the knee or a head lock to bring them down."

"Keep in mind that it is important for you to be at the front of the crowd by the time you reach the bottom of the steps," said Mr. M-1. "For those who will be climbing the walls, the goal is to be at the base of the wall with no crowd in front to prohibit your climb."

"I must say that I am impressed," said Mitch. "I've been doing these gigs since the beginning, but I never realized how much planning and organization goes into the success."

"This one is definitely the 'super-bowl' for us," said M-3. "Before this we had other things happening that distracted from our political purposes. The 'smash and grab' operation took a lot of the heat. Also, the Antifa faction and BLM faction had their own agenda. The violence and destruction they fomented took a lot of pressure from us. With this 'Capitol' gig, we're basically on our own. It'll be a delicate balance, but we can pull it off. We don't want to destroy the place or burn it down. If we do this right the news media will be talking and writing about it for years. It will look like a Trump rally that got out of control. It should change the course of history.

Mitch sat for a moment and absorbed all of this. As he realized the importance of his part his self-confidence began to slip.

"What happens if something goes wrong, and it all comes apart?" he asked.

M-1 and M-3 looked at each other and paused before M-1 answered, "Let's put it this way, if that happens, I wouldn't want to be the cause of it."

CHAPTER 4

After they relaxed and enjoyed the hotel amenities for the rest of the weekend, Mitch, Bolo and Dinny met the three Russians. There were some apprehensions to overcome at first since this was a new experience for all of them. As they worked through the dry runs that were a part of their mission training, they got more relaxed with one another. There was a personality conflict involving Dinny and the Russians, however. They were a little resentful when Dinny, with his lower mentality, got a little 'bossy' with them. Those who knew Dinny overlooked this trait and laughed it off. Mitch had to take the Russians aside and explain this to them. This eased the tensions.

Dinny was able to show his worth as a driver. He was able to negotiate the rush-hour traffic with ease, and once he looked at a map, the route was imprinted in his brain. Everyone was pleased with how well the dry runs went and Mitch pronounced that part of the preparation a 'go'.

Oreo and Bones went to meet up with M-1 and M-3 for instructions on their objectives when they reached the Capitol. While this was happening, Mitch worked with Bolo, Tats and the two substitutes that would be under his supervision. The new guys were both big men. Mitch felt a little awkward being the leader of this band of giants, but he took comfort in that none of them were *mental* giants.

The plan called for the two imported men to return to M-1 and M-3 after they left the Capitol, while the three Russians stayed with Mitch. When all the details were worked out, they were good to go.

Late Tuesday afternoon, Mitch had a meeting with his five charges. He set the time he expected them to be ready the next morning. He could rely on Bolo and Dinny to be on time, but he wasn't sure about the others.

"I am required to make a report to the Chairman, the man in charge of all of this, about the performance of my men. I know you want to 'party' this evening, and you have certainly earned the right. Don't screw up by being late or hung-over. That wouldn't look good in the report."

That seemed to get through to them as they went off like a group of teenagers on a field trip. Mitch was sure they would all be seeking female company while they tested their limits of alcohol consumption. Personally, he opted to pass on the opportunity this time. He would do his celebrating when the mission was completed, and the pressure was off.

Mitch spent the remainder of Tuesday making sure the gear was in the van and everything was ready for a smooth departure. After that he went to his room and tried to relax. It was a failed effort. All he could think about were the countless things that might go wrong. It was well into the night when he finally got to sleep.

CHAPTER 5

January 8, 2021 – Columbia, South Carolina

John Osmond was packed and ready to leave the Army post at Ft. Jackson, South Carolina. He had spent the last night bunking in the quarters of a friend and saying his goodbyes to some co-workers at a party in his honor. He had been discharged from the Army the previous day.

He had met many new friends over the past twelve years since he made his commitment to life as a soldier. One of the unfortunate aspects of that life, however, was that those friendships were short lived. They were often limited by the duration of each new posting. John's limits were defined even more minutely since he was a part of the Special Forces.

By definition, the Special Forces have nine doctrinal missions: unconventional warfare, foreign internal defense, direct action, counter insurgency, special reconnaissance, counter terrorism, information operations, counterproliferation of weapons of mass destruction, and security force assistance.

John had entered the R.O.T.C. program at the first opportunity when he started his college studies. Upon graduation he went directly into the Army to fulfill his obligation to Uncle Sam. His test scores were high enough that he got to choose what he wanted to do in the military. He had completed Army basic training during the summers while in college and had chosen his career path during his senior year. With college diploma in hand and the rank of 2nd Lieutenant he went directly into Special Forces training.

It was hard work, but John had the body and the mindset to succeed. Upon graduating he proudly wore the Green Beret, the official headgear of Special Forces. Over the next few years, he performed some of his country's most difficult work and was stationed in some of the world's worst regions while he did it.

John remained single while he served and had no burning desire to change that. He saw how difficult balancing marriage and parenthood was for some of his friends and decided to forgo that challenge for a later time in his life. He also recognized the risk of having fate intervene and taking him out before his time. He felt the greatest compassion for the widows and children of his fallen comrades.

Now, after twelve years of his life working toward a career in military service, John found himself single and an unemployed civilian.

"Thanks Tracy, for allowing me to bunk here during my last night in government housing. It certainly beats staying in a motel," said John.

"It was an honor to have you John," said Tracy. "I will long remember sharing my humble abode with one having such a distinguished military career, and if that doesn't satisfy you, I can feed you an even greater line of BS."

"What you can feed me," said John, "is one more wonderful meal in the officer's mess. You're buying."

"It will be my pleasure. I can buy you a meal since you saved my 'bacon' more than once. What time does your ride get here?"

"Roger will be picking me up at 8PM," said John. "His wife, Judy is attending some big librarian conference in Chester and he's on his way up there to bring her home. I can't imagine what they have to confer about unless it would be to find new and innovative ways to say, 'Quiet, please'. He'll drop me off at a truck stop along I-75. I'm supposed to hitch a ride with a freight hauler friend of mine who will meet me there and take me on into Jamestown, New York."

"That should be an interesting trip," said Tracy. "I sure hope this 'Jamestown' thing works out for you. You've had some tough breaks lately. You'll land on your feet. What you're looking for is out there. Keep trying."

John and Tracy enjoyed their dinner and spent the balance of the time talking about old times, especially the good ones. They were through some rough patches together, and there was no need to think about them. Surprisingly, Roger showed up promptly at 8PM driving a red Mustang convertible. He was not famous for being on time, but he *was* famous for having classy cars.

After John and Tracy said goodbye and promised to keep in touch, Roger and John headed north. They spent the first part of the trip on debating the attributes of the Ford Mustang vs. the Chevy Corvette. Roger was a car nut. After that they talked about their college days. They got to John's designated truck stop and parted. Roger went on his way and John waited for his next ride.

CHAPTER 6

January 8, 2021, Gainesville, Florida

Karen Grant checked and double-checked her list. She wanted to be sure she went over every detail of her current patient care status with her assistant, Joyce. Karen was getting ready to leave on a two-day weekend.

"Don't worry so much Karen," said Joyce. "We have it under control. What I don't remember, Robin will. She's coming along well, and she has good retention. She'll be up to speed in no time. If we get stumped on anything, we'll phone you. Relax and enjoy your break."

"I guess you're right," said Karen. "I worry too much. Maybe Ernie will show up. It's about time for him. If he does, tell him I'm sorry I missed him."

Ernie was a regular patient. He showed up every couple of weeks and kept the nurses entertained. It was helpful to have somebody like that to balance out the crotchety ones they seemed to have a lot of.

Karen was proud of the seemingly unending reserves of strength she could call on. In nurse's training, they called her "super-girl." At 5' 10" tall Karen had a slender but muscular body that was topped off with thick curly blond hair. She liked to style it long like most of today's TV personalities, but that did not work well for a nurse. She styled it in a tight bun, that made her look even taller. Her co-workers called on her when they needed help moving a heavy patient, or when they needed to intimidate an uncooperative one. She got all of that, including her good looks and winning smile from her mother, Martha.

By the time Karen got going, rush-hour traffic had subsided. She made it home to her apartment in good time, with just a quick stop for some carry-out food. There would be no cooking tonight. A hot shower, then early to bed would prepare her for a much-needed two-day break. Karen had made no plans for her weekend, as she had been so often required to cancel them as of late. The work demands at the hospital had been unrelenting for much of last year due to Covid-19. Scheduling the nursing staff had to be a nightmare for her boss. Nurses who had young children were faced with suddenly having to deal with home schooling. Some older nurses made the decision to retire, often on short notice. The profession had suddenly become high-risk. For many of her coworkers, the world was turned upside down. At age 28 and single, Karen currently had no attachments.

After nurse's training she continued her education on an accelerated basis and got her nursing degree. Karen's time-off often disappeared when she was called upon to fill-in for someone who had a scheduling problem. She did so as often as possible. Being a nurse, compassion for others was ingrained in her. It was so hard to say "no" when her friends were in need.

The phone was ringing as she got out of the shower. "Probably another telemarketer," thought Karen. She was going to turn off the phone when she got home, but she forgot. Caller ID said it was her mother. "Hi, Mom, what's up?"

"Oh Karen, I was just about to give up. I was afraid I was going to miss you, and I *really* need to talk to you."

"I was in the shower, Mom, and I can't hear the phone when I'm in there. What's wrong? You sound upset."

"It's Kurt. He has the virus. So far, he is just weak, with a slight fever and a weak cough. I put him to bed and called Sheila. I told her not to come over, and to keep the kids at home. I told her to call off work and self-quarantine for all next week until we see if she was infected. She can cancel the daycare for the kids and have a little personal time with them. She should be able to get tested relatively quickly considering the circumstances. I'm a little flustered with all this. Can you think of anything else I should be doing?"

"You usually have oranges on stock. If so, give him all he wants of those, and orange or cranberry juice if you have any. Vitamin D is supposed to be good to combat the virus. I will bring a supply with me when I come home. I'll call you again before I get there to see if you need anything else. Zinc is also supposed to help."

"Now Karen, don't be silly. You're not coming up here! It's a two-day drive. I can handle this. Don't forget, I'm a nurse too."

It's not the nurse part that concerns me," said Karen. "What if Sheila is infected? Who will take care of the kids overnight? There is also the small matter of the farm to run. Don't argue with me on this, Mom. I'll call you after I get on the road. I'm on my way. Bye.'

Karen's Dad had passed away three years ago around the time she was in the process of finishing her schooling. She took a little break to help her mother adjust to the change. Her brother Kurt was a big help. He was two years younger, and he seemed to welcome the challenge of showing his big sister that he was ready to be the man of the house. He adjusted his life to take up the slack in the farm chores and fill the void left by his father's sudden death. Kurt had the family work ethic, and he quickly learned to balance being a husband and the father of two young pre-school children with being his mother's strong helping hands on the farm.

"At least I don't have to change clothes," thought Karen, as she stood naked, drip drying onto her bedroom carpet. She dressed quickly in some comfortable travelling clothes. Tired as she was, the family emergency gave her a shot of adrenaline and helped her fly into organizing her thoughts for her trip to Pennsylvania. As she packed her clothes and some snacks for her trip, she placed everything by her apartment door. She grabbed her medical "bug-out bag" that contained first-aid supplies, and most recently some added supplies for dealing with covid-19 patients. She also slipped her Smith & Wesson 9mm M & P (Military & Police) Special into the bag. Karen had a concealed-carry permit. It is valid in most states. She wasn't sure about Virginia, but she hoped not to test that on this trip. The gun has a laser sight and is a good fit for her hand. She has a steady shooting hand and has acquitted herself well on the range. Karen wasn't fanatical about carrying the gun, but travelling the long distance by herself, she felt more comfortable having it with her. When everything was loaded into her car, she watered her plants, locked the door and headed out.

When she was clear of the city, she settled into a comfortable drive through some of Florida's most beautiful farm country. Even in winter's early darkness, she let her thoughts wander to memories of the family farm, her destination, where she and her brother spent their childhood. She phoned her Mom to see how she and Kurt were doing.

"Kurt had a nap and didn't have any appetite for dinner, but I did get him to drink some juice as you suggested. He has his cell phone under his pillow so Sheila can keep in contact with him. Since you would be driving, I told him to text you so you could return his message when you stopped for a break. I'm not real big on texting, but I'll call you that way also. Oh, I wish you weren't making that long drive by yourself."

"Time is of the essence Mom. There was no time to consider any type of public transportation, and I do not know anybody who could travel with me at the drop of a hat. Besides, what better way to get a break from the hospital. I plan to see that Kurt gets well and to enjoy my time at home. Oh, I almost forgot, I need to call my supervisor and give her the good/bad news. I'll talk to you in the morning. Bye."

Karen continued east across Florida toward Jacksonville and points north. She had a text from Kurt around 10PM. She pulled over at the next rest stop and had a voice conversation with him. They agreed to work together to help their mother get through this. The plots and conspiracies of children. Some things never change. Kurt is a strong, healthy young man and Karen expects that he will be over the effects of the virus in a few days.

Kurt had followed in his father's footsteps in the farming business. While dad was alive, Kurt kept his hand in by helping a few days per week in his off time from his regular job as a school bus driver. This job was basically a part-time job, but it involved having to work a split shift. He had early morning runs and he had afternoon runs. Between them was a hiatus that allowed him enough time to do some farm work. The farm work was not too demanding on him early on, and he found time to get married and to start his own family. When dad took sick, however, he helped his mother with the farm more and more. It was after Kurt's first child was born that his father died. Frank Grant got to see his first grandchild. After his passing, Kurt worked the farm as much as was necessary and the bus driving job became second priority. Kurt's supervisor, Erik Johnson was very understanding and scheduled him all afternoon runs for his bus driving duties.

CHAPTER 7

It seemed to take forever to get through Georgia. Caffeine worked for a while, but the greater consumption of liquid necessitated more rest stops. When ya gotta go, ya gotta stop. Karen was reminded of the story of a couple who wore adult diapers to cut down on their cross-country travel time. This was not for her. By the time she passed all the exits at Columbia, South Carolina, she was exhausted. Struggling to keep the car on the road, she pulled off at an exit that had one of the large truck-stops.

After the rest room and a quick sandwich to go, she walked through the exit doors and promptly tripped over something on the sidewalk and fell to her knees and hands. Her ego was bruised more than she was, but she still tried to look around to see if anyone observed her moment of grace. Before she could stand fully erect, she was surprised by a pair of strong arms helping her to her feet. "Are you okay?" He asked. "I saw you start to fall, but I couldn't get to you in time to catch you."

"I'm okay, thanks. I'm more embarrassed than hurt, and more tired than either of those."

"Let me help you inside to a table where you can sit for a while. It will help keep that knee from stiffening up if you can move it while you sit." he said.

After she was seated, she looked up and was rather surprised to see what looked like an Army recruitment poster. He was tall; about 6' 2" with dark hair and rugged good looks. He was wearing an Army uniform with Captain's bars and all kinds of badges and decorations. His name tag said "OSMOND." He appeared to be about 30 years old. After what was a long pause, she thanked him for coming to her assistance.

"It's not often a lady as pretty as you will *fall for me*. Let me get my luggage before it walks away", he said. "May I sit with you? It's getting a little chilly outside and I'm afraid I didn't pack my overcoat. I'm John Osmond."

"I'm Karen Grant," she said. "I hope my clumsiness didn't cause you to miss your ride."

"On the contrary," he said. "I just gave up on my hope of getting a ride to New York with a freight hauler friend of mine. I don't know what happened, but I got stood up. He must have had a good reason. Knowing him, he probably lost my phone number. How far do you plan to drive with that injured knee?"

"I was hoping to continue into south-western Pennsylvania," she answered. "I hope this doesn't force a 'plan-B.' I hadn't planned on an overnight stop. Will you be able to get to your next duty station on time?" she asked.

"I sure will," answered John. "I'm in no particular hurry because my next duty station will be as a civilian. I do not have to punch any time-clock."

"Should I? or shouldn't I?" thought Karen. "He certainly appears to be an 'officer and a gentleman', and I need a break from the demands of the road."

Before Karen could put her thoughts into words, John made the offer, "It's a little presumptuous of me to ask, but would you be willing to let me drive for you? It appears to me that you want to keep driving without stopping for the night. I'm well rested right now, and you could get a break. If I drive to I-79, that will give you about four hours to rest. If you dropped me at a convenient spot, there, I will be able to continue to western Pennsylvania and to my goal of Jamestown, New York." Karen was hesitating and pondering John's offer. John took out his wallet and showed Karen both his military and civilian drivers licenses. "Perhaps I should tell you a little more about how I became stranded in 'Podunk', South Carolina," said John. "Until about a year and a half ago, I was planning a career in the military. My widowed mother lived near my last duty station, Fort Jackson, in Columbia, South Carolina. She had failing health, and I was able to provide for both her personal and financial needs. That responsibility put a strain on my deployment responsibilities. The Army was cooperative as much as possible, but I could see that my career acceleration had stopped. Mother passed away two months ago. I had already decided not to reenlist when my present time expired, so, after twelve years on active duty, I became a civilian yesterday. Mother had accumulated considerable medical expenses prior to her passing, and I was able to pay all of them as well as her funeral expenses. I sold my car to get enough for clearing all of that. So, here I am, basically trying to hitch rides to Jamestown. One of my friends has arranged a job for me in his family's business there."

"Wow! It looks like you have had a lot to deal with," said Karen. "Your travel route coincides with mine for most of the way. It makes sense that we can travel together. It's not that much different than if we were meeting while travelling on a bus. My reason for wanting to hurry is that I have a family emergency that just developed. I'll tell you about it on the way."

As they walked to Karen's car, John told her he would buy the gas for the rest of their trip. "I may be temporarily down on my luck, but I'm not broke," he said.

"You don't have to.....," started Karen. But John insisted as he hoisted his travel bag into the car. Karen was limping a little, but her knee didn't seem to be badly hurt.

CHAPTER 8

As they got back onto I-77 and headed north, Karen observed that John was careful to keep his speed to just over the posted limit. She was pleased with this considering that she wanted to hurry, but not at the expense of caution. At first, they didn't talk. Karen observed that there was no wedding ring on John's tanned hands. There was no pale skin to show evidence that one had been recently removed either. "Oh, stop it Karen," she thought. This was no time to be looking for a romantic encounter.

Karen was the first to speak. She told John about her mother's phone call and how she jumped into action to get headed to Pennsylvania. She was wide awake now, but it probably wouldn't last. She told John that she was a nurse and worked at the hospital in Gainesville. She gave him a brief explanation of her family ties to the farm in Pennsylvania, telling him that her mother would be overwhelmed by these events without her help.

John listened attentively as Karen enlightened him as to her plight. When she slowed down and he could tell that she was quickly tiring, John told her a little more about himself. He had served one tour in Iraq and one in Afghanistan, with duty stations stateside in between. Most recently his last duty station was at Ft. Jackson. His job in the Army was classified in nature, and he couldn't go into much detail of what he did. Karen noticed that one of his ribbons was for a purple heart. She asked him about that. John replied that he had been hit in the leg by enemy fire. Thankfully, the wound had not been debilitating, and he has suffered no permanent damage.

"Dad was wounded in Vietnam. He had to have some recuperative surgery at the VA Hospital in Pittsburgh after he was discharged from the Air Force. That's where he and my Mom met. She worked there as a nurse after her schooling."

"What did your dad do in the military?" asked John.

"He was in the Security Service. Like you, he couldn't talk about what he did, and it was not until after the fall of the Berlin Wall we learned that he could speak Russian! Imagine keeping that to yourself for all those years. I looked up 'United States Air Force Security Service' on the internet. It said that the work they performed was largely declassified after the Wall came down and the Soviet Union broke up. The story went on to give a detailed account of their mission during the Cold War. It was impressive. Dad told us a little about it after that. He lost much of his language ability through lack of use. There was not much opportunity to use it on the farm, as the cows were not able to understand."

After that, they engaged in small talk until Karen began to fade rapidly. She drifted off into a deep sleep as John continued to drive northward.

Karen had reclined the passenger seat to get as comfortable as possible. John took the opportunity to further appreciate what a good-looking woman she was. Having to spend much of his off-duty time with his mother, he was not accustomed to having an encounter with a classy woman like Karen. She had dressed her shapely body in a way that enhanced it, but somehow did not make her look cheap. She wore no rings at all. That could mean that she was not spoken for. It could also be a convenience of her nursing duties. Rings and rubber gloves do not go well together. Her skin did not have much tan, but that was probably due to the disaster that 2020 was for those in the medical professions. It had been a long time since John could even think about being around a woman like this, and here was one, only a few inches away. He let his mind dream about additional encounters.

"Keep your mind on the business of driving, John," he thought. "This is no time for wishful dreaming."

CHAPTER 9

January 7th, Hagerstown, Maryland

Mitch was driving west on I-70 in the Ford Econoline van with his motley crew. They were all road weary from a day of intense traffic following their gig in D.C. To look at them as a group, one would think they were a rock band. They were dressed like "hippies" from an earlier time, and they were on the run. Everything was quiet now, but usually all of them were arguing and bickering about something. They had stopped at a rest stop and tried to get some sleep in the van, but that did not work out well. Besides Mitch, there were five others in the extended length van. It was starting to smell.

They finally decided to get a couple of motel rooms and get some sleep before the next leg of their journey.

Bolo wanted to stop in western Pennsylvania to pick up some gear from a cousin of his. The guy worked in a gun store and could get what they needed. None of them could pass a background check. They were paying a steep price for the stuff, but they could afford it. The stop would take them a little out of their way, but they had time for it. Maybe Bolo's cousin could find them some chicks and a place to crash for a while. They still had plenty of time to get to Michigan for their next gig.

Mitch was reminiscing about the job at the Capitol as he drove. The crew was dressed much like the others in the huge crowd of protesters gathered in D.C. A couple of them wore MAGA hats and they had a Trump flag on a short pole. They had blended in perfectly with the rubes that had come in support of Trump. The crowd hung on the President's every word as he spoke. When his speech was finished, he had told them to walk peacefully to the Capitol to impress the seated senators and representatives.

Mitch and his gang had dropped back and picked up some additional gear from their van. They carried some tools that would help them complete their mission of breaching the Capitol perimeter and gaining access to the inner chambers.

They had reentered the crowd and made their way to the front, where they muscled through the perimeter guards. Tats had gone up the steps with Mitch and Bolo, while Bones and Oreo proceeded to climb the walls. Those two gained access from a balcony. Somebody from another group had broken out some windows, and they climbed through to the inside.

They did their thing once inside the building. None of their previous jobs had gone this well. When the cops finally started to overcome the masses that had broken in, Mitch's group had hightailed it out without a scratch. They ditched some of their gear when they got outside. They all made it to the van without incident. It was great.

The plan was to go back to their hotel and spend one more night there before heading north toward their next gig. They encountered a lot of foot traffic congestion, followed by some crowded streets on their way back. When they got there, they covered the things in the cargo area of the van before entering the hotel. They wore jackets to cover their 'costumes' so they wouldn't stand out from the rest of the hotel guests.

Theirs was a quiet celebration that evening. They didn't mix with some of the others in the hotel who had also been a part of the Capitol breach. This was a dangerous time for all of them. Until they got out of D.C., they were at risk of being photographed by security cameras. (They were everywhere). There were also the TV cameras as well as untold numbers of civilians with their cell phones. The success of their mission depended on strict security measures. This event was going to have more attention from the media than anything in recent history.

The 'volunteers' who joined in with them when they rushed the Capitol were one of the best parts of the plan. They were the fervent believers in their party's cause, and in the heat of the moment they would expose themselves to the cameras and to law enforcement. This took the attention away from the planned activities. It was expected that this directed attention would continue well after the actual event.

Mitch kept his thoughts to himself about how things played out politically. The second impeachment effort had begun and was following along as planned. The public thought they were crazy to be pursuing this, considering the President would be out of office by the time any trial was completed. While all eyes were on this, his group would quietly leave D.C. and head north for their next project.

When they checked out of the hotel the following morning, they quickly switched their Georgia plates for Pennsylvania plates, since they would be headed north out of the city. It was a little tense until they got through the traffic. Then they were on I-70 and home free.

CHAPTER 10

The miles melted away as John drove them through North Carolina and on into Virginia. Karen slept the entire time, until she was awakened by the noise of a large truck grinding up a mountain a little south of the I-81 intersection. "Welcome back," he said. "You were really in dreamland for a while. You missed North Carolina completely. The traffic around Charlotte was not so bad this time of night. I haven't been through here for a while. The new high-occupancy lanes must have made a big improvement. I remember my last trip through there was at rush hour and it was awful."

"I know, said Karen. I always plan my travel to miss rush hour at Charlotte. I also wish I could stop there and enjoy the area. I especially like the Lake Norman views."

"This is the first time I have been through there after dark. The lake and the lights certainly are beautiful," said John. "Maybe when I make my fortune, I'll retire there."

Karen laughed. "If there is only one lakefront home left, you'll have to fight me for it. I always think that too. "When we come to the jointure of I-77 and I-81, I would like to stay on I-81 for a couple of miles past where they separate again. This is a little off course for us, but I usually like to stop for gas at a Sheetz store there. A fill-up there will get me all the way to the farm."

"What's a sheets store?" asked John. "Do we need to pick up some bed linen?"

"Do you mean to tell me you don't know about Sheetz stores? You're in for a treat. They usually have the best prices in the area for gasoline. Their convenience store is second-to-none, and their deli food is somehow always fresh. A farm family in the Altoona area of Pennsylvania started the chain. They have expanded to over 500 stores in several states. We can gas-up, and then both go into the store for the rest rooms and some food. I'll show you how to navigate their touch screen ordering system. Start thinking of what you want to eat. They probably have it."

"I was starting to get a little hungry," said John. "Now you have intrigued me, I'm anxious to try this place." Karen offered to take the wheel, but John said he was still doing well. She could take it for a while in West Virginia. They could stop somewhere in the Route 19 shortcut for her to take a turn. Karen was pleased with this, as she planned to take another nap. When she got to the farm it would be like working another double shift.

When they got to Route 19, the starting and stopping at the many traffic lights got Karen awake again. They decided to stop for a comfort stop when John spotted the familiar red canopy of another Sheetz store. They were becoming like an oasis in the desert for him. He hoped they had them in Jamestown. John took the wheel again, and they decided he would drive as far as Morgantown, where they would part company. He was not looking forward to that, as he had become comfortable having Karen next to him.

CHAPTER 11

Mitch's crew was getting restless now. Dinny had been feeling sick for the last hour, and he seemed to be gradually getting worse. Bolo was telling him to "man up," that they didn't have far to go before they would stop for the gun buy. Bolo's cousin would know where to get some help for Dinny. They had left I-70 and headed into farm country a while back, and there didn't appear to be any place they could stop for help. "Stop. I'm going to be sick!" said Dinny.

"Yeah, stop," said Tats, "We don't want him barfing in the van. It smells bad enough in here now." Mitch was the boss, but Tats was the biggest and the meanest. If possible, Mitch went along with him and avoided controversy. Mitch was small, but he was smart. He pulled off the road. They practically had to lift Dinny out of the van, where he promptly threw up into the weeds.

"He's burnin' up," said Oreo. "We best be gittin' away from him before we all gets it. It probly be da virus. I don't want none a dat!"

"There's a farm up ahead, "said Mitch. "We'll pull in there. If the layout is right, we may be able to hole up for a while to work this out."

CHAPTER 12

Mitch had pulled the van into the driveway at the Grant's farmhouse. He drove it just a little past the front door, so the rear of the van was visible. He had a "Clergy" bumper sticker on it. This was to confuse law enforcement when he was on the highways, but it served his purpose here as well. He got out of the van and walked up to the front door and knocked.

Martha came to the door and looked out through the decorative glass and saw Mitch. She saw the back of the van and noticed the bumper sticker. Feeling at ease with that, she opened the door to Mitch.

"Hello, I'm Reverend Bradley Pogue. I wonder if you could help me. One of my group has taken ill, and we're not familiar with the area. We may need to find a hospital or an urgent care facility."

"Well, the nearest hospital is about five miles from here. I can direct you there. Let me look at your friend. I'm Martha Grant, and I happen to be a registered nurse."

"Why thank you Mrs. Grant. We appreciate your kindness. Are we interrupting your lunch? I wouldn't want to keep Mr. Grant waiting for his meal. Farmers like to keep on schedule."

"That's true, but you are not interrupting anything. It's just me and my son here and he's resting right now. I suspect he has come down with the virus, so I won't invite you in. Let me get my mask and my medical kit. I'll come out to your van and we'll see if I can be of help."

Mitch (Rev. Pogue) sneaked a quick look into the living room as Martha had turned and entered another room to get what she needed. Martha returned with the medical bag and accompanied the Reverend out to the van. He slid open the side door and stepped back so she could see Dinny, who was slouched in the near seat. Then she saw the rest of the passengers, who were all staring at her. Her first impression was that the Reverend must be ministering to a group of recovering addicts. She was a bit taken aback by their appearance, but none-the-less she proceeded to check on Dinny. His temperature was 104° and he seemed to be short of breath. Martha had one of those new miniature EKG monitors, so she tested him with it. His heart rate was a little elevated. "It could very well be the virus, with his symptoms. Of course, I can't be sure with what I am able to test here. You should probably get him to the hospital."

"Your son must be in better condition than Dinny then?" Asked Reverend Pogue. "If you are able to care for him here, I mean."

Martha was beginning to feel that something here was amiss. "Yes, you're right, he is doing well in his recovery."

Before she could say anything else, Reverend Pogue quickly said, "You are obviously a qualified nurse, Mrs. Grant. I think we'll take you up on your offer to treat him here, in your house." By that he opened his jacket enough so that Martha could see the gun he carried in a shoulder holster.

CHAPTER 13

Martha had stood there wide-eyed when she saw the gun but did not show fear. After a few seconds, she said, "I assume you are *telling* me rather than *asking* me, Reverend, if that's what you really are."

Mitch could see that he would have to be careful with this woman. She had backbone. "Boys, carry Dinny into the house. Mrs. Grant will tell you where to put him."

Two of the men lifted the sick one out and carried him into the living room. Martha had to think fast as to what to do next. She told them to hold onto him for a couple of minutes while she got a bed ready in the next room. "That's where my son Kurt is, she said. Let me go in first, so I can keep him from getting upset. If this is going to be a damned hospital, we may as well make that a semi-private. Excuse the language, *Reverend*." Martha's thoughts had been that they would want her tending to their virus patient, and if he were in the room with Kurt, she could keep an eye on him also. They probably didn't give a whit about Kurt.

"Go with her, Bolo. See that she does what she said." As Martha entered the other room, she noticed that the other two from the van were coming into her living room.

Kurt looked up and saw the rough looking stranger with his Mom and noticed the concerned look on her face. He started to get up, but Martha quickly put her hand on his chest and held him back. "No, son," she said. "Do not interfere. We have some uninvited visitors who have brought one of their own, who has the virus, into our house. They will not hurt me if you keep calm and stay in here." Before Martha removed her hand from Kurt's chest, she

45

tapped him with her finger six times. "They will be bringing my new patient in here to keep you company." Martha quickly turned down the other bed and started out of the room.

Kurt told her to be careful. He also told Bolo that if they hurt his mother, he would kill them. Bolo laughed at the empty threat as he left the room. Tats and Bones carried Dinny into the room, stripped him down to his underwear and put him into the bed. They each gave Kurt menacing looks as they left the room.

CHAPTER 14

Karen stayed awake this time and they talked during that last leg of their journey together. She was having similar thoughts about enjoying her time with John. They had been driving about two hours since their last stop, when Karen got a beep on her phone that she was getting a text. That was probably from Kurt. She gasped when she read the message. "What's wrong," asked John.

"Kurt says, '6 bad gys, 1 sick with vrs, frcd Mom to tk in & help. Txt me b4 u arv here 4 sitrep. K'. I don't know what to do. Kurt probably thinks I stopped for the night and am a day away from them. Should I call the police to get them some help, or would I be putting them at risk? This is a kidnapping. Anything could happen!"

"I would say your thoughts are right on target. We need more information. Text him back and ask if they are armed, and where they are in the house."

Karen did that and got an immediate answer. "ys. All r rmd. 1 n my rm, 4 n ktchn, 1 tkn van into brn, lks lk pln to sty awl. K."

She read Kurt's reply to John. He thought for a minute and told her to tell him, "back to you in 10." She sent that out to Kurt as John pulled off the road.

"We need a plan. First, I'm going with you. We need to have eyes on their position and find a way to separate them. Divide and conquer. It's a classic hostage rescue scenario. I am familiar with how to go about this with minimum exposure for your family."

"John, I can't ask you to get involved with my problem. This is dangerous, and it is not your responsibility. You would be risking your life. I just can't let you do this."

"I've done things like this before, many times. No argument please. We don't have time for that. Once we assess the situation, we will be able to better decide how to get law enforcement involved. What kind of police force to you have?"

"The local force is small, and is in Mount Pleasant, about three miles away. The farm is not in their jurisdiction, but I'm sure they would respond in a serious situation like this. The state police have jurisdiction, but their barracks is about twenty miles away. One of the officers in Mount Pleasant is a high school classmate of mine. If I could talk with him directly, I'm sure he would take every precaution to protect my family. He could bring in the state police more effectively than we could. I have his sister's number in my directory. I'll call her and find out how I can get in touch with him on the job."

"Good, do that, but first text back to Kurt that help is on the way. Don't give him any more information now. This is for his own safety and for the safety of your mother. We don't want them doing anything to try to help that might be counter to what we will be doing. I'll punch in the address of the farm to the GPS, then we can step on the gas and get there as quickly as possible. The big hemi engine in the car will be a help in getting us there more quickly." Karen's car was a well-appointed Chrysler 300.

CHAPTER 15

"There is something important I should tell you, John. I have a gun with me." Karen reached behind the driver's seat and hefted her bug-out bag up into her lap. As John pulled back onto the road, she showed him the weapon.

"We may need that before this is over, said John. I assume you have a concealed-carry permit for it."

"I do, said Karen, and I know how to shoot. I don't want to shoot anybody, but I'm sure I will be able to do it if it becomes necessary in this situation."

"Let's keep it in that bag for now, and not on your person. That way, either of us can get to it if necessary. I assume there is a full clip loaded into it and one would need to rack the slide to make it hot. Is that correct?"

"Yes. That's the way I was trained. It sounds like you know this model." said Karen.

"You might say so. I carried one just like it as a back-up when I was deployed. I still own it, but unfortunately, it's in storage back in Columbia. Since I was going to New York state, I wasn't confident about taking it with me on my trip. I know that New York City is very touchy about guns. I don't know anything about the rest of the state. Tell me about the layout of the farm."

Karen was successful in getting the contact information for her police friend. She and John each put it into their phones, to be ready to call when the time came. She felt sorry for

Kurt that she had been so brief in her message to him. He must be climbing the walls. For the better part of an hour Karen explained details of the farm buildings, the house and the grounds surrounding all of it to John. He interrupted often with questions to help clarify things for him. By the time they turned onto the road leading to the farm, he had a good mental image of it all. As a last-minute thought, Karen got out her wallet and showed John pictures of both Kurt and her Mom, so he could quickly recognize them if necessary. She also got her extra set of car keys out of her purse and gave them to John. The car could be available to either of them if they were separated. They rounded the last bend. The barn came into view, as John pulled slowly off the road into a stand of trees.

CHAPTER 16

John walked across the black-top road that fronted the farm buildings. He entered a thicket of sumac bushes and wild blackberry bushes that separated the fenced pasture field from a dense wooded area between the Grant farm and a neighboring property. He had stopped at a rest stop earlier on I-79 and changed from his uniform into a comfortable flannel shirt and blue jeans. His uniform would have suffered badly in the thorny dense bushes. He wore his army boots also. He didn't know what he would be needing in Jamestown, but he had packed carefully in his one piece of luggage. He would be able to dress for a job interview and for some apartment hunting if he were successful with the interview. Thoughts about Jamestown were not remotely in his mind now. He was laser focused on the mission of helping Karen's family. John found what was probably a deer trail that he could easily traverse through the woods. He stopped briefly to send a text to Karen with a *situation report*. They had agreed that she would wait in the car until they decided on how to approach the problem. He decided to use voice for this call, as he was far enough away to speak softly and not be heard. John was looking at the ancient barn as he called Karen. The boards were vertical and almost black from weathering. There was some spacing between them that Karen told him he could use to peek inside. "Karen, I see the end of the barn details as you described."

"Do you see the larger door that the cows use to enter for milking? To the right of it is a small man door that you can use to gain access. Find a thin stick that you can slip between the boards and lift the latch. The door is rarely locked from the inside. If you look through several places and don't see anybody, you can slowly open that door and enter. I hope the hinges do not squeak. Keep to the right and watch where you step. Most of the droppings will be to the left where the milking area is. The stalls ahead of you are for calves. They should be empty now. Look along the front wall and you will see the ladder to the upper level. There are a couple of rooms on the lower level, opposite the end where you entered. They should be empty now but be cautious. Carefully climb the ladder and listen for noise on the upper level. If it is quiet, raise your head above floor level and look around. Shut your phone off then and call or text me when you are safely in the upper level. We don't need to be interrupted by a call from one of your admirers right now."

"No need to worry. I'll turn it off." After determining the lower level was clear, John entered and found the ladder. He climbed about half-way up when he heard a noise coming from the upper level. He froze and listened intently. He heard it again. After the third time he heard a snort that was probably not human. He climbed up and peered over the top. There was a large, enclosed stall in the far, right corner in front of him. There was an animal in it. He couldn't tell what. Looking to the left, he could see a large extended body van parked just inside the sliding barn doors. In front of him was a huge vat of some kind, with a belt-driven motor at the bottom. This must be the grain grinder Karen had told him about. Other than that, he could not see any human presence. There was a lot of clutter that probably was indispensable on a farm. John made his way carefully to the far end of the barn, peeking carefully in the van windows to be sure it was unoccupied. He found another room, at the rear corner, that he found to be empty. More clutter, of course. Looking out through a large knothole he could see the end of the farmhouse. It was about a hundred feet away. Unlike the barn, it was pristine. He could believe that a woman like Karen was raised in a house like this.

He stepped back to have a closer look at the enclosed stall. There was a carefully lettered name on a varnished board. Apparently "Jake" was in the stall. John stood on his toes and peered carefully over the top board. Jake was right in his face looking back at him. He was probably not the largest bull he had ever seen, but it seemed so at the time. John fell backwards from the shock, and almost lost his footing. Jake gave a couple more snorts to express his feelings about John.

"Karen, I'm on the upper floor now and everything is quiet. I met Jake however, and he is a little intimidating."

"Oh! I'm sorry John. I forgot to tell you about him. There should be a barrel of oats near his feed box. Just give him a scoop and he will be your friend for life. Can you see the house now? The right corner window is in the room where Mom probably has Kurt and the unwanted visitor. Are the curtains open or closed?"

"I can see the house. The curtains are mostly closed. That's perfect. I should be able to get a peek into the room without being spotted. I see the spring house you told me about, located about half-way between here and the house. There are some high bushes along the driveway that should give me some cover when I approach the house. I'm going to try to get close enough, …. wait, there is someone headed toward the barn. It looks like one of the visitors. I'm going to hide now and find out what he's up to. I'll get back to you."

The man was average in height and a little pudgy. John watched him as he entered through the sliding doors and raised the hood of the van. He tinkered with it for a while and went to get a wrench from the large mechanic's toolbox near where the van was parked. It must not have been the right size, because he took it back right after he tried it. He f shed around in the group of wrenches until he found another one. This one worked for him. He proceeded to remove a spark plug and looked carefully at it before wrenching it back into place. Next, he went to the back of the van where he opened the sliding barn doors about half-way. He then got into the cab and started the engine. He revved it for a minute or two and shut it down. He seemed to be satisfied with his work, since he closed the hood and turned toward the rear of the van. He opened a rear door and rooted around in the back cargo area. He came up with a screwdriver and a Michigan license plate. Next, he removed the Pennsylvania plate from the van and installed the Michigan one. After that he put the Pennsylvania plate inside, replaced the screwdriver and closed the door. He then turned and started to leave the barn.

The floor of the upper level of the barn was covered with a thin layer of hay and straw, obviously accumulated from what dropped from the bales as they were handled. This gave John the advantage of stealth. He silently crept up behind the man and tapped him on the shoulder.

"Who the hell are you?" said the man. John answered him with a right cross to his jaw. He was out cold. John found some rope in the tool area and hog-tied the man securely. He used the rag the guy had for cleaning his hands to gag him. Too bad. He had some experience on how to deal with prisoners. He called Karen back and told her what had happened. She was a little flustered with that news, but recovered quickly, realizing that this was to be expected. John asked her where he could stash the guy where he would be out of sight and not be heard.

"There is a chute from that level into the lower level near the grain grinder. Slide him down that. You should be able to drag him into one of the calf stalls and cover him with some hay to muffle any sound he might make. What happens next?" asked Karen.

"They won't be expecting him back right away since he was working on the van, so I'll do my snooping now. If I get stranded, my next call may be a text if I have to hide." said John.

"Those bushes along the driveway are thornless berry bushes and they are very dense. You should be able to work your way into them if necessary. Please be careful."

The driveway came up along the far side of the house to a fork. Straight ahead it continued into a field, passing two machine sheds along its course. The left branch of the fork passed the back of the house, the back porch alcove, and continued to the back of the barn and the dirt ramp to the 'upper-level' sliding doors. John slid the doors open enough to get through and closed them behind him. He walked uprightly, at a normal pace toward the house. To hurry and to crouch, as would be the normal tendency would most certainly make him look suspicious. That could get him shot. He was mostly hidden by the berry bushes and the spring house. He kept his eye toward the back porch alcove for any sign of movement. He also checked on the position of the window curtains to see if anybody was looking out. This was the most dangerous part of the mission so far. He wondered if the Grant's had a dog. Most farms did. It was a bit late to be thinking about that now. When he got to the corner of the house he turned right and crouched under the first window. According to Karen, that one was in a pantry, and should not be a problem. As John approached the other window, he noted that the drapes were thick and would probably keep his movement from being seen. The open gap was about an inch wide. He carefully looked crossways through the gap and found that the window was behind the heads of two twin beds. The door to the room was closed, and all was quiet. A man occupied each bed. He couldn't see much of their faces, but he saw enough to determine that one was blond and clean shaven while the other had dark hair and a beard. Kurt and the visitor with the virus.

John made his way back to the barn safely and hopefully without being seen. After checking on his prisoner and finding him awake but unhappy, he called Karen. "You guessed right about the room. Kurt is in there along with one of the bad guys. They both appear to be sleeping. I forgot to ask if there is a dog in the house. That can be a problem if my presence is announced."

"No, we lost our old black lab a couple of months ago. He would probably have heard you too. He didn't have many teeth remaining, but his sense of hearing was still excellent. Mom decided to wait until spring to get another puppy. Old Harvey would not have liked the visitors pushing their way in. He was very protective."

Now it was time for the part of the mission John was not happy about. It was time for Karen to go into action. He searched his brain for any scenario where he could keep her out of it, but there was just no way. He had a plan of how to divide the enemy forces, but Karen needed to be an integral part of it. John hoped to further diffuse the situation until they brought in the police. The kidnappers must be desperate to do what they did. It was still a mystery why, but John had a couple of ideas as to their motives. "Karen. Are you ready for your move?" he asked. "I want to get you in place before the others miss their mechanic and come looking for him. He didn't have a cell phone on him, so that is a real possibility."

"I'm ready, John. Don't forget, we both have the contact number for my policeman classmate in our phones. His name is Jose' Cantina. You can count on him for help."

John and Karen had formulated a rough plan on their way to the farm. It involved Karen driving in and acting surprised at the situation. She would enter through the back door, as was her custom. The guy in the barn would not be expected to hear her arrive, nor would the sick guy. John would send a text to Kurt and a message that Karen was on the scene, and to remain alert, as he may need to disable the sick guy if things got dicey. He was told to be ready to assist, but not to act on his own without being called to help.

Karen pulled out of the hiding spot and onto the road. She turned into the driveway and drove past the end of the house to the back porch area. She was careful not to show it, but she noticed somebody looking out the living room window as she passed by. She had her concealed carry purse with her as she got out of her car. The gun was in the part that opened from the end. She had pushed it in as far as possible and put a small baggie full of tampons in to help hide it. Hopefully, anybody searching her purse would not notice the side compartment, and if they did open it, would not see the gun. She had a worrisome thought as she passed the front of her car. "What if they check her car and discover that the hood is cold?" she thought. "Too late to be concerned with that now."

CHAPTER 17

"Mom, I'm home," said Karen as she opened the outside door to the kitchen. The expression on her mother's face as she entered the kitchen from the living room told Karen a lot. She could tell that her Mom was concerned, but not overwrought. As she got the welcome hug from her mother, she set her suitcase down and got her first look at one of the men. He was standing in the archway between the rooms with a menacing look on his face as he stared her down. "Who is your guest, Mom?" Karen asked in a joyous manner.

"Oh Honey, I'm surprised to see you so early. We weren't expecting you until tomorrow. This man calls himself Reverend Bradley Pogue, though I suspect that is not his real name. His associates call him 'Mitch', and he is an uninvited guest."

"What do you mean? Mom. What's going on?"

"What she means young lady, is that my loyal followers and I are resting here while your mother cares for one of my flock who has come down with the virus. We're pleased that you have come to help." With that, another of the men appeared in the archway and stood behind Mitch. He was huge, with tattooed arms that he proudly displayed in a sleeveless shirt. While Mitch was smiling when he spoke, this big one was scowling at her.

"Where's my brother, Where's Kurt? I want to see him." Now there were four men standing in the archway.

Martha answered her this time. "There is one more in the guest room with Kurt. This man has a bad case of the virus, and it is best that you do not go into that room without observing hospital protocol. Kurt is doing much better, but he still needs to be isolated. Oh, there is another one who, for some reason left and went to the barn."

"Now that we all understand each other, Mrs. Grant, why don't you invite your daughter into the living room," said Mitch.

"Why don't we drop the fake formality, Mitch. My name is Martha, and my daughter is Karen. Do what they say Honey. Let's try to cooperate so this will be over soon."

Karen gave Mitch a threatening look and said, "Look mister, I don't know who you are or why you came here, but this is my mother's home. You can't just push your way in here and make demands. Why is it always little guys like you who like to push women around?"

Mitch got red in the face, and said, "Now Karen, your mother just gave you good advice. Now zip your lip! If you want to see what it's like to be 'pushed around,' I can introduce you to Tats here. He would enjoy showing you some, wouldn't you, Tats?"

The big guy smiled at Karen with his mostly toothy grin. The threat was plain. Karen could probably squash Mitch, but this big oaf was another story. And there were still two more of them in the room. She would keep quiet.

CHAPTER 18

"You gave her good advice, Martha," said Mitch. He had dropped his fake smile. "Tats, take Karen's purse and show her into the living room."

The big guy took her purse and looked inside. He put his big grubby paw inside and rooted around a little, and was apparently satisfied, dropping it onto a coffee table. Karen waited until the others took seats so she could sit by herself, as far from any of them as possible. She gave a silent sigh of relief that he hadn't found the gun. Mitch went over to a photo display on the living room wall. He pulled off one of Karen in her graduation nursing uniform. "I see you are also a nurse, Karen," he said. "Like mother, like daughter they say. I wonder if you both can cook. The boys are getting a little hungry. It's well past their feeding time. What do you say, Martha?"

"Come on Karen, you can give me a hand," she said. "If we feed them, they might be a little more agreeable."

Mitch followed Martha and Karen into the kitchen. "What's on the menu?" he asked.

"We always have eggs," said Martha, "and beef. I can slice some beef and make you steak and eggs."

"That sounds good to me," said Mitch. Martha started to go into the pantry to get what she needed. Mitch told Bolo to go with her.

When they came out with what she needed, Bolo said, "Just food and cooking stuff, Boss." Bolo joined the others in the living room and Mitch took a seat at the table where he kept a watchful eye on Martha and Karen while they prepared the food.

They ate like pigs at a trough. Table manners were in short supply, and when they finished, a couple of them let out loud belches. While that may be a sign of appreciation in some parts of the world, it was not the standard of etiquette expected in Martha's kitchen. She didn't even like it in the barn.

Mitch told Martha what a fine meal that was and his companions all grunted their approval. Martha's comment was that it took work and money to provide that much food, and that his group had made a large dent in her household food budget.

"I understand Martha. Cough it up boys," he said. Mitch reached for his wallet and took out a brand new twenty-dollar bill and laid it on the table. Each of the others followed suit. Three more new twenties appeared on the table.

"Whatever they were, they weren't cheap," thought Karen. "It's time to gather today's eggs before it gets to be milking time," she said. "After that, the eggs need to be processed and packaged. Mom has a local egg route that she does twice a week. She will be expected tomorrow. If she doesn't show up, the phone will start ringing. In another hour, she will need to milk Daisy. If she doesn't get milked twice a day, every day, she will set off a racket you could hear a half mile away. This is a working farm. Schedules must be kept."

"I get the point," said Mitch. "Bolo, help Martha get the eggs and bring them back here. I'm curious to see how they are 'processed' before they are boxed."

As Martha and Bolo set off toward the barn, Karen busied herself with cleaning the kitchen. "I'm back in western Pennsylvania now", she thought, "and I can start working like it." The ever-present Mitch sat at the table and watched her like a hawk. She couldn't get a message to John, as her phone was in her purse in the living room. She was sure John would see them heading his direction and would secure himself before they got near the barn. The henhouse and nesting areas were outside, in the pasture area just above the end of the barn. They had no reason to enter the barn and see him.

"Where do you live, Karen?" asked Mitch. "Your mother was surprised to see you, so it must not be nearby."

Karen saw no reason to be deceptive, so she answered, "I live and work in Florida. I came here because my brother got the virus and I wanted to help Mom with the farm chores."

"I see," said Mitch. "I noticed by the pictures in the living room that he has a family. I suppose they live somewhere else. Why do you suppose his wife hasn't phoned to see how he is doing?"

"Nothing much gets by him," thought Karen. "Kurt's wife gets home from her job soon," said Karen. "She will pick up the kids from the day-care. I'm sure she will be calling Mom for a report on Kurt. She doesn't much like being separated from him by the virus, but what choice do we have."

"Right," said Mitch. "This virus has been hard on a lot of folks, but except for poor Dinny in there, it has been good for us. We get lots of security work from it."

"What exactly do you do?" asked Karen. "Your friends do not exactly fit my idea of security people."

"Well, we are, and we get lots of good paying jobs. Before the virus hit, most of us were good-for-nothing bums," said Mitch. "Now look at us."

"Yeah," thought Karen, "not *most of you,* all of you." "You should let Mom talk to Kurt's wife when she calls. She'll know how to handle the call."

When Martha and Bolo returned with a good supply of brown eggs from their free-range hens, Martha placed the two baskets on the counter in preparation for cleaning and candling.

Mitch watched carefully as Martha did this. Then he asked Karen if she knew how to milk a cow. "Yes," Karen quickly answered. This is what she had hoped for. She could communicate with John if she could get to the barn.

Mitch said, "Great! Bolo. Take a break. Tats. Go watch Karen do the milking. Maybe you can learn something."

Karen would have much preferred that Bolo accompany her, but the die was cast. She would have to go with Tats. Hopefully, John could help her if Tats got out of hand with her. She set off for the barn with the milk pail and with Tats following behind like a huge puppy dog.

CHAPTER 19

Karen saw Daisy headed for the barn, right on schedule for her milking. Karen went to the lower-level door so Daisy would see her enter. The big jersey cow went right to her milking stall and to her feed box. Karen scooped some grain into the box and grabbed her milking stool. She got right to it, just as if she had never left the farm. Some things you never forget. She talked gently to Daisy as she proceeded to fill the pail with milk. Tats stood back from this process and quietly observed. It was obvious that he had not been around a cow before, because he seemed to be in awe of this animal that was considerably larger than he was.

Daisy's tail swished contentedly as she ate the last of her grain and Karen finished up. Daisy backed out of her stall and went to a feed bunk at the end of the barn. Karen hefted a bale of hay and dropped it into the bunk. A gentleman would have offered to help her, but Tats was no gentleman. Karen told him she had to go to the upper level to feed another animal. She went to the ladder and started to climb up. She could feel Tat's hungry eyes on her butt as she climbed up. He was right behind her as she reached the upper level.

As Karen stepped away, Tats reached out and grabbed her from behind. She let out a little yelp and tried to release his hold on her. As she tried to twist away from him, he changed his position and kept his hold on her body. "Come on little lady, you know you want it. I've been watching you," said Tats. As Karen struggled harder to get out of his grasp, she was surprised to hear what sounded like a 'clang' from behind her.

Tats suddenly let go of her and nearly fell to the floor, but not quite. John had hit him over the head with a shovel, but not hard enough to take him out of action. Tats shook his head back and forth as he blubbered a threat to John. As his vision cleared, he came up with a knife in his hand and went after John. This startled John, who had already set the small shovel down, thinking it had done the job. John was smaller than Tats, but he was quicker. He stepped away from the thrust and was trying to think of what he would do next in the fight. Karen handed him a long-handled hay fork.

With all this action in his domain, Jake went into a frenzy. He began to snort and to shake his huge head in protest. He sensed the violence, and he didn't like it. John had an idea. He began to move his footing as he and Tats parried for position. John got him positioned so that his back was to the door of Jake's stall. Then he gave a couple of quick thrusts with the fork that backed Tats into the door. It stopped Tats for an instant, but then gave way and came open as the latch broke off.

Tats fell backwards into the stall where Jake was waiting for him. He was treated with a head-butt to the ribs that threw him against the wall of the stall. Jake twisted his huge body a full 180 degrees and followed up with a two-legged kick that snapped Tats' collarbone and laid him out cold on the floor. Jake stood over him with his nostrils still flared.

"That's enough Jake!" said Karen. Her voice seemed to immediately calm the animal. She went into the stall and without fear, walked up and put her arm around Jake's neck. As Karen whispered sweet nothings into Jake's ear, she motioned for John to drag Tats out of the stall before Jake could finish him off. With some cautioned steps, John slowly entered and grabbed Tats by his feet and dragged him to safety. Karen then stepped out and joined John as he closed the stall door behind her. Karen found some zip-ties that were used to close feed sacks. They put a couple of those in place to hold the door closed until the latch could be repaired.

"That was amazing, Karen. I never would have believed you could handle that animal the way you did. Weren't you afraid?"

"Jake and I are friends," said Karen. "We grew up together. He wouldn't hurt me." Karen examined Tats while he was still unconscious. He had at least two broken ribs and a broken collar bone. There were also some abrasions on his head where he smashed into the wall of the stall. They decided it would be best to tie him securely, thinking that he might still be a handful, even with injuries. When they had him hog-tied in the same fashion John had used on the first guy, they lowered him down the grain trough into the lower level. John dragged him into a separate calf stall from the one he had used before. They covered him with plenty of hay, thinking he would probably be moaning from the pain when he came to.

With business taken care of, Karen threw her arms around John's neck and gave him a fierce hug. "That's for saving me John," she said. "I don't want to think about what might have happened without you and Jake being my rescuers." They held each other for a long time before Karen let go of him. "I should be getting back to the house," she said. They quickly came up with a reason for Tats' absence that would be plausible. They also came up with a plan to lure another of the visitors to the barn. "Divide and conquer," said John.

"I don't think it will be long before Mitch sends another of his men here to see what is keeping the two missing ones. You should get ready as soon as you can," said Karen.

"I have an idea for a way to create a distraction that will help me take out the next one," said John. "I'll be ready for him. Oh, by the way, while I was waiting here, I had a little time to explore. I looked in the van, and what I saw gave me a good idea of what these jerks have been up to. I'll fill you in when we have more time."

John opened the sliding doors enough for Karen to slip out carrying her pail of milk and slid them closed behind her. He headed immediately for the ladder to the lower level. John went down and into the stall with the first man. He removed the hay that covered him and began to untie part of the rig that secured him. The man looked up at him and tried to speak, but the gag prevented that. John worked quickly and without comment. First, he removed the man's boots. Next, he unbuckled his belt and started to pull his pants down. With this, the guy began to protest by making noises around his gag and twisting around as much as he was able. John silenced him by holding up his fist in a threatening manner. He finished removing the pants and re-tied the hog-tie rig. He gave the guy a friendly pat on the cheek and covered him again with hay. With that part of his plan being completed, John took the boots and pants up the ladder to the upper level of the barn.

There were several bales of hay stored near Jake's stall. He talked quietly to Jake as he worked. They seemed to have become friends. According to what Karen had told him, the pants belong to a guy they called, "Oreo." John stuffed the legs of Oreo's pants with enough hay to make them look like his legs were inside. The pants were a kind of pumpkin color. The others should recognize them as being Oreo's. Next, John took the pants over to the rear of the van. He carefully slid them, waist first, under the van. He then put the boots on the fake legs by sliding the cuffs over the boot tops. He stood back and looked at his work to determine if it looked natural. He made a couple of minor adjustments and went to the next step. He got the jack and raised the rear of the van enough to make it appear that Oreo was working on the rear-end. He then looked at his work from just inside the sliding doors. That being acceptable, he looked again from the area at the top of the ladder from the lower level. Either way the next man entered the barn, he would see what appeared to be Oreo under the van. The plan was not foolproof, because he didn't have a fake Tats in it, but it should get his next victim in place.

John next chose what would be his hiding place, one that would allow him to surprise the next victim from behind. Then he went to his usual knothole to watch the house. He didn't have long to wait. He saw another man heading toward the barn. He was alone.

CHAPTER 20

As Karen walked back to the house, she thought about what she would say when Mitch confronted her about the missing "Tats." She had no more got into the kitchen and set the pail on the counter when Mitch appeared in the archway from the living room. "Where's Tats?" asked Mitch. He gave her a look as if she had taken his favorite toy.

"It's not my day to watch him," said Karen. She immediately regretted the smart answer when Mitch raised his hand to slap her. She was saved by Martha, however who had just entered the kitchen to take care of the milk. Mitch obviously didn't want to tangle with both Grant women.

"Don't give me any lip, Karen," he said. "Why didn't he come back with you?"

"Oreo asked him to help with something he was working on with the van. I don't know what he was doing. I'm no mechanic. It was something at the back of the van. I told him I had to get the milk processed, and he sent me back to the house," she said. Karen didn't like playing the 'dumb blond,' but she could do it when she had to.

Martha had her back to them as she poured the milk slowly into glass jars, straining it through a white cloth. "What are you doing now?" Mitch asked her.

"I'm straining the milk," answered Martha. "It will contain impurities from the milking process. Bits of hair from the cow will fall into the pail. Also, some dust in the air will get into it. This straining will make it clean and safe for consumption," she said.

Mitch called "Bones" into the kitchen and told him to go to the barn and find out what was going on. "I don't like this," said Mitch. "It shouldn't take that long to clean the plugs. Something else must be wrong. This doesn't smell right. Tell them to get back here. Bring some beer from the van. There doesn't seem to be a drop of it here."

Karen could see Bones as he left the house and walked toward the barn. His skinny body seemed to be too loosely connected and he kind of swayed as he walked. What a strange bunch.

Bones slid the sliding doors open and looked carefully into the barn. He took a tenuous step inside and spotted the fake legs under the back of the van. He said, "Oreo, Shto voi tam deleate! Mitch rastroeya, kak boichok." (tr. *What are you doing there? Mitch is upset, like a little bull.)*

John was almost in shock. He hadn't heard any Russian since he was deployed to the outer reaches of Afghanistan. He certainly didn't expect to hear it here. As he was processing this, he heard Bones say, "Gdeh Tats? Shto on deleat? Mitch skazaet:' totopitsy, eali voi razreshite!, e prinocit piva." (tr. *Where's Tats? What's he doing? Mitch says 'Hurry. And bring beer.')* Bones stood quietly and scoped-out the room. There was no sign of Tats and Oreo was not responding. He slowly took his gun out of its shoulder holster and looked all around him. After a couple of minutes, he relaxed somewhat, holstered his gun, and took out his cell phone. He speed-dialed Mitch. "There's no sign of Tats and Oreo is under the back of the van. He must be passed out or something. I can't get him to answer. What should I do? Do you mean, just leave them here? Okay, this is on you if the Boss doesn't like it." Bones disconnected the call and turned his back to John's location. John sprang from his hiding place wielding his trusty shovel and bashed Bones over the head with it. Three down. "Now what do I do," thought John. "This is an entirely new wrinkle. Bones and Oreo are probably both Russians. Probably Tats is too. But since Bones spoke English on the phone call to Mitch, he must not be able to understand Russian." As he worked to get Bones securely bound and gagged, he mulled over different ideas as to how to proceed. He knew he was working against the clock. Even though he could only hear one end of the conversation, he surmised that Bones was planning to take the van and go up to the house. After that, one could only guess. None of the guesses were good. John stashed Bones in the last calf stall, removed the fake pants and boots and this time waited in the lower level. He got into position, removed the shoulder holster rig and the semi-automatic that Bones carried, but the holster rig was too small for him, so he just carried it all with him. He found a place where he could see through the cracks in the boards well enough to get a view of the back of the house. He didn't have long to wait again. He was just cutting it too close. He sent a quick text to Kurt telling him to play sick.

CHAPTER 21

Mitch had just disconnected the call from Bones and turned to Bolo with an angry look on his face. "They're missing. Both of them. Those damned Russians are more trouble than they're worth. We're getting out of here." Mitch then turned to Martha and told her to get into a closet.

"What are you doing," she demanded. Karen started to come to her defense when Mitch drew his gun and pointed it at her. He told her to sit down and shut-up and her mother would not be hurt. Karen reluctantly complied. "What about Kurt?" asked Martha. "I need to check on him. He's not recovering the way he should be."

"Don't worry about him," said Mitch. "If he needs anything, Karen will take care of it." Karen couldn't figure out what was going on, but she could sense something bad was about to happen.

Mitch braced a chair against the closet doorknob to keep Martha from getting out on her own. He then turned to Bolo and told him to try to get Dinny on his feet and bring him out into the living room. Bolo headed into the guest room, helped Dinny get dressed, and soon returned with him being partly carried and partly dragged. He put him into an armchair and went back to close the door.

"Karen, I need you to listen carefully. Bolo and I are going to leave you alone here with Dinny for a few minutes. Your brother is in his room and your mother is in that closet. I expect them to be there when we get back. If they're not there, or if you try to do anything stupid, somebody will get hurt. We will be leaving in a few minutes for good, so do as you're told, and this will all come out okay."

Mitch and Bolo went out the back door, with Mitch giving Karen a warning look as he exited. After a couple minutes she went through the kitchen and into the pantry, where she could safely watch them as they quickly headed toward the barn. She turned and hurried back to Kurt's room door, noting that Dinny was still slumped in his chair. She opened the guest room door a little and looked in. "Kurt," she said quietly, "Are you awake? We need to talk."

CHAPTER 22

Mitch and Bolo slid the upper doors open full width. Guns drawn, they stepped into the barn and quickly looked around. "Back the van out", Mitch said, "I'll watch here till you are turned." When the van was out and pointed in the direction of the house, Mitch quickly got into the passenger side, and they headed up the drive to the house.

John was kicking himself. He had positioned himself in the wrong place. He had hoped for the confrontation to take place in the barn, where he knew the layout. He wanted them both to be in the upper level where his approach would give him an advantage. That turned out to be a bad plan. They moved too quickly for him to get at them without dangerously exposing himself to two guns. He headed for the ladder to the upper level and went up to figure out his next move.

CHAPTER 23

When Kurt heard Karen's voice, he turned cautiously to look out the door. When he saw that she was alone he bounded out of the bed to embrace her. This is the first time they had been able to greet each other since this fiasco began. He got John's short message of caution and played his part while Dinny was being removed from the room. He started to get a little dizzy as they stood there in the doorway. He had been off his feet for a long time, and even though he was feeling stronger, he still fell short of total recovery.

Karen told Kurt about them locking Mom in the closet, and that she believed they were about to leave. She thought it best that he stayed in his room on alert and be ready to continue playing his role if they checked on him. If they locked her up, he could free both her and mother after the bad guys bugged out. Kurt heard the engine approach and peeked out his window in time to see the back of the van head behind the house. Karen went back into the living room and he closed the door, wishing that he were well enough to be able to help more.

CHAPTER 24

Mitch and Bolo hurried back into the house. Mitch looked around and saw that Karen was calmly seated on the sofa. The chair still held the closet door closed. He walked over and pounded on the door with his fist. "Martha, are you okay?" He asked.

Martha answered through the door that she was okay, but not happy about being locked up in her own house. Mitch told her to be patient a little longer, that this was almost over for her.

"Okay, Karen," said Mitch. "Get your jacket and help Bolo get Dinny into the van." Bolo and Karen maneuvered Dinny through the kitchen and out the back door to the van. Mitch had opened the sliding door and they slid Dinny into a reclined seat and buckled him in. This was the same way he was when he came to the farm. If he was improved, it was only a little.

"Okay, both of you come with me," said Mitch. He walked around the van to the other side door and opened it. "Get in!" he said to Karen.

Karen was stunned with the realization that they planned to take her with them. "I'm not going with you!" she said. "You don't need me along. I would only slow you down."

"Except for one thing," said Mitch. "Dinny still needs you to help him recover." With this Karen started to struggle to get away from Bolo who was prepared for that. He and Mitch forced her into the seat beside Dinny. Mitch took a plastic zip-tie from his pocket and tied her hands together. He then took another one and tied them to the handrail on the back of the front seat.

Karen told Mitch that she needed her purse. She said she had tampons in it that she would be needing.

"Bolo, get Karen's purse," said Mitch. As an afterthought he said for Bolo to also get her bag with all her nurse's stuff in it.

Bolo got into the front passenger seat and put the bag and Karen's purse between Mitch and himself. Mitch pulled forward and turned the bend leading to the road. He then turned and went north, heading for their next destination.

CHAPTER 25

It took John a moment to process what he was seeing. When it dawned on him what was happening his reaction was minor panic. By the time John made it through the lower level, up the ladder and out through the open doors, the van was just pulling out from the back of the house. He hurried to the house as fast as he could but was too late to catch up to the van. It had already cleared the house and was turning onto the hard road. John gave it everything he had as he reached the far corner of the house. He could see Karen through the window in the side door of the van and saw her looking back at him. John's heart broke.

CHAPTER 26

Kurt had been listening intently at the door of his room and had heard Mitch, Bolo and Karen leave through the kitchen door. He couldn't hear any conversation after that, but when he heard the van start up, he cautiously entered the living room. Finding it empty, he checked the kitchen. He looked out the outside door the saw that the van had left. He heard the engine accelerate as it started up the hard road. He could see Karen looking out the side window of the van. As his shoulders slumped a man placed his hand on one of them. Surprised, he turned quickly and looked into the face of John.

Kurt and John each immediately figured out who the other was and quietly entered the kitchen. "Oh," said Kurt, "I have to let Mom out of the closet." Kurt quickly entered the living room and removed the chair from the closet door.

When Martha came out, she said "What a relief. I was starting to get claustrophobic." She looked at the new face and said, "You must be John." She looked at the two worried faces and quietly asked, "Where is Karen?"

Like Kurt, Martha could hear conversations in the living room through her closet door, but when the group left the house, she no longer knew what was happening. Kurt was first to speak. He said, "I'm sorry Mom. By the time I could leave my room, they were already pulling out. I had no idea they would take her, or I would have tried to stop it."

"Mrs. Grant, It's not Kurt's fault. If it's anyone's it's probably mine. I should have positioned myself better in the barn. I just couldn't get here in time. That they took her was also a surprise to me."

What happened next showed what courage Martha truly had. She said, "It was nobody's fault. It surprised all of us. There was no good reason for it." She then took both of her arms and put both her son and John in a double hug.

When the tension had eased a little John said, "I'm going after her Mrs. Grant. I don't know how yet, but I'm going to bring her back."

"John, if we're going to work together on this, you need to start calling me Martha. What kind of idea to you have? How can Kurt and I help?"

When John's brain hadn't been occupied with the family scenario, he was quickly beginning to devise a plan. "First, I have an idea where they might be headed," he said. He told them what he had found in the van during his time in the barn. "Michigan is their likely destination. That means they will probably be travelling on the Ohio turnpike. That gives me a good chance to catch up with them. One thing that would help me a lot would be if I could use Karen's car. It has that big Hemi engine and that would give me an advantage of being able to quickly shorten the distance between them and me. Our last fill-up was in Wytheville, so it must be getting low."

"I'm sure Karen would want you to do that, John," said Kurt. "We can help move things along a little for you. I'll fill up the gas tank from our farm tank and save you that stop."

"While Kurt is doing that," said Martha, "follow me and I'll take you to our armory. I have something a little better for you than that handgun you have. Where did you get that?"

"I took it from one of the guys in the barn," he answered. "I did not travel with my own weapon. It's a piece of junk, but it's all I have."

John followed Martha upstairs and down the hallway to the paneled end wall. She placed her hands on the wall about three feet apart and pushed upwards. That loosened a large section of wall that she lifted aside. John was surprised to see a large gun safe inside the hidden area. Martha worked the combination and opened the door. Inside was an impressive collection. There were half a dozen shotguns, about a dozen rifles of various sizes and calibers, and nearly a dozen handguns. On one end wall was a supply of ammunition and various accessories.

As John stood open mouthed at what he was seeing, Martha said for him to take anything he wanted. She handed him a shoulder holster rig and told him, "This belonged to my husband, Frank. He was about your size, so it should fit you." She then handed him a 40 caliber Glock semi-automatic pistol. "This was his favorite. It is well oiled and ready to go."

John accepted those, and selected a 12-gauge semi-automatic shotgun, a Colt AR-15 rifle, a short barreled 9 mm S & W revolver, a hunting knife, and a pair of binoculars.

As John took those down to the back door, ready for loading into the car, Martha filled a tote bag with a supply of ammunition for the guns. Kurt was back with the car, and as he and John loaded the gear into it, Martha was preparing some sandwiches for the trip.

While she was finishing this, John and Kurt talked outside. "I want to go with you John. Karen is my sister and I want to help," said Kurt.

"I expected you to say this Kurt," said John. "But for several reasons, I don't think this is a good idea. First, you have a young family that needs you. Secondly, your mother needs you here on the farm. This could be dangerous. Next, I need you to deal with bringing in law enforcement to take control of the guys in the barn. Also, I'm a professional. I have done this kind of thing for the past several years. It would be the first time for you, and with Karen being your sister, you might not be able to think objectively in a tense situation. I have several good contacts among my past friends. I'm sure I will be able to get help if it is needed. I hope you understand. Also, Kurt, the ideas you came up with are going to be a big help to me in this mission."

Kurt looked dejected but recovered quickly. He and John stepped back into the kitchen and the three of them said their goodbyes. John told Kurt to call their friend, Jose' Cantina right away and give him the whole story. He would be able to decide what agencies to bring in. John asked that Jose' call him right away so they could establish contact in the matter of Karen's rescue. John promised to give them periodic progress reports.

John grabbed the food Martha had made for him and hurried to the car. He didn't waste any time getting out the driveway and onto the road. What they had been doing in preparation for his departure had seemed to take forever, but it was all necessary. He reflected that his encounter with the Grant family was certainly an exciting and meaningful experience thus far. He only hoped and prayed that this would continue.

CHAPTER 27

When John and Kurt had paired John's cell phone to the car, John's contact list was automatically in the system. All he had to do while he was driving was to switch the system into play and give a voice command to call the desired number from his contact list. He decided to make his first important call right away, to get his friends involved in helping to find Karen.

John's friend Harry Lemack was a go-to guy. Usually, every outfit in the military had one of those. He was the guy who could cut through red tape to arrange anything. He could get you something you needed when all other efforts failed. In situations like that, when you resorted to Harry after being frustrated with by-the-book attempts, you learned to just go to him straight away and not waste time. After John learned this, he just went directly to Harry when he had a difficult problem. This one would be a real challenge for Harry. John needed a helicopter.

When he left the farm and drove north, John had only a slim lead to go on. The switch to Michigan license plates on the van was that lead. He could guess the route they would take, but that would be like looking for a needle in a haystack, even though the extended van was not that usual of a vehicle. A 'chopper' would make that search much easier and faster.

John tried Harry's home number and was talking to him after only two rings. As usual Harry was sitting at his computer. John told him the whole story, from the time he met Karen up to the present. He was careful to explain what led him to suspect that the bad guys were likely connected to the Russian mafia, and that they were probably involved in the breach of the U.S. Capitol. He was sweating the little detail that he was no longer in the army, but Harry was already on top of that. Harry was conversant with all the 'alphabet' government agencies and

John didn't know which one he would choose. It turned out to be Homeland Security. He could get a chopper in the air, flying eastward along the Ohio turnpike from Toledo. If it came upon the van that way, it would not alert them of a search the way it would if he approached from their rear. If they took another route, which was unlikely if their destination was Michigan, then it would be back to the drawing board. Harry would call John when he got the search lined up.

CHAPTER 28

John made his next call to Kurt at the farm. He wanted to reassure him and Martha that he was making progress and that he would be keeping them informed. John learned that Kurt had called Jose' Cantina, their friend in the Mount Pleasant police department. He had arrived promptly along with his partner. They uncovered the hog-tied men, removed their ropes and zip ties and replaced them with handcuffs. They read them their rights and took them into custody. Jose' said he would be calling in the state police since the crimes took place in their jurisdiction. Kurt gave Jose' John's cell number. He could expect a call from the state police when they became involved with the case. Kurt had to chuckle a bit. Jose' told him that all three of the prisoners immediately told him they had to use the bathroom. Jose' told them they would have to 'just hold it.' They had already caused enough crap at the farm

Except for being anxious about Karen, both Kurt and Martha seemed to be holding up well. John told them there would be more reports to follow.

CHAPTER 29

Karen was scared. She had never been in a situation that caused her fear to the extent this one did. She quickly made up her mind, however, that she would not show her fear to her captors. She sat quietly in the back seat and set her mind to the task of trying to help herself get out of this fix. After a few minutes she was distracted by Bolo when he grabbed her purse and started to root through it. He noticed the side opening and unzipped it. He removed the bag of tampons and put his hand inside the deep pocket of the purse. He came out with her gun!

"Well, lookie here!" he said as he held up the gun and showed it to Mitch. "Our little honeybee has a stinger!"

"That stupid Tats missed that when he searched her purse earlier," said Mitch. "Good riddance to him." Mitch took the gun and stuffed it into his pocket. Then he asked Karen, "What were you planning to do with this?"

She answered, "I always take it with me when I travel. You never know what kind of people you are going to run into."

Mitch mulled that over for a while before he said to Bolo, "I think that was an insult! And after all we've done for her." They both laughed.

"Where are you taking me?" asked Karen.

'You'll find out soon enough," said Mitch. "You just look after Dinny. If you need anything out of this bag of goodies, let Bolo know and he'll get it for you. In the meantime, you can rest and enjoy the ride."

It was dark now, but Karen could recognize most of the places they passed. After all, she grew up here. Mitch had told Bolo to call his cousin. Karen could hear one side of that conversation. The cousin was someone named 'Phlegm.' What strange nicknames this group had. She couldn't wait to see what Phlegm looked like. She wondered if he would look like the disgusting bodily fluid she saw as a nurse. Bolo arranged to meet Phlegm at a small house with several outbuildings that was located off the track of their present route.

When they arrived at the meeting place, Mitch and Bolo got out and left Karen tied to the seat back in the van. She tested the security of her ties once they had left but found them too tight to make any headway toward freeing herself. They had left her bug-out bag between their seats, but no matter how she stretched and turned, she was unable to retrieve it. There were scissors and a scalpel in the bag. If she could only reach a little further, she could cut herself free.

They were in the house for what seemed like an eternity, but it was probably only about fifteen or twenty minutes. When they returned there was another man with them. This was probably Phlegm. Each one was carrying a canvas bag about four feet long. They appeared to be heavy. Mitch opened the rear doors, and they stored the bags in the rear cargo area of the van. When they finished, the new guy looked in the side window of the van and saw Dinny. "He doesn't look so good," he said. "What's wrong with him?"

"He has the virus," said Bolo. "He's holding his own, Phlegm. He even has his own nurse." Mitch and Bolo snickered.

"Why in hell didn't you tell me," he shouted. "Now I could be infected!"

"Don't get all bent out of shape Phlegm," said Mitch. "We have been careful around Dinny. We didn't hack or cough in your place. You should be okay."

Karen didn't correct Mitch. In reality, they would all be lucky to avoid the virus after riding together in an enclosed vehicle. As a nurse, she took the suggested precautions, but when she was thrust into her present situation, that became beyond her control.

Phlegm had calmed a little. He looked across the van at Karen and said, "Too bad she's been around the virus. I could've spent some quality time with her."

He was not so bad looking like his name implied, but Phlegm was still not her type.

They exchanged a few words outside the range of Karen's hearing. After that Mitch and Bolo got back into the van. This time Bolo drove. Karen didn't like this, as she imagined a long trip was in store with the driver change. They soon got to I-70 and took the ramp heading west. Karen wished she had been able to spend more time talking with John about his ideas on what the group was up to.

CHAPTER 30

"When are we going to stop?" said Karen. "I need a rest room." She had come up with an idea that she planned to implement when they stopped, and she hoped it would be sooner rather than later.

"We'll stop at the next rest area," said Mitch. "Take care of business while we're there because we won't be stopping again for a while. We have food in the back that we got from Phlegm. Do you like survival food?" he asked.

"I don't know. I've never had the pleasure," said Karen. At this point, she thought it better to keep her conversations with them brief and to the point. "Survival food," she thought. "Any food she could get right now would become survival food."

CHAPTER 31

John was moving at a good pace on I-70. He had to decide if Karen's captors would be travelling north, and then west. Or they could be going west and then north. He didn't even know that. His intuition had not let him down in the past, and he hoped and prayed it would work for him now. He was basing his pursuit on the license plate change to a Michigan plate, and the fact that he had seen the van leave the farm heading north. He also had a feeling that these guys had been involved in the breach of the U.S. Capitol building on Wednesday. They were heading north to get to western Pennsylvania. They stopped at the farm with a sick man. John had also seen Georgia plates and registration papers in the back of the van. The only central theme he could come up with using that data is the Capitol. Georgia, Pennsylvania and Michigan fit the puzzle in that they were all states where rioting had taken place. Since the presidential election, and its unbelievable result, political analysts had been suggesting a connection among these events.

John had reached the point of his choice of route. He chose I-70, the interstate route that would take him due west. There were several alternatives from I-70 to take him north to connect with the Ohio turnpike. He figured the jumping off point to be Toledo. That would lead to Detroit. Other exit points would be plausible for direct routes to other Michigan locations. John's gut was telling him Detroit.

"If only," thought John as he crossed into Ohio on I-70. "If only I had beat more information out of Oreo, Bones and Tats." At the time he believed he could wrap up the mission at the farm. He'd had a good plan. It had reached the point where it could be wrapped up. John could now see the couple of things he could have done differently that would have made the outcome better. He had learned through many past experiences that it didn't pay to dwell on those mistakes. His thoughts were interrupted as his phone rang.

CHAPTER 32

The call was from a man named 'Todd Farley.' He identified himself as an agent of Homeland Security. Harry Lemack had come through again. John could hear engine noise in the background. Todd told him he was in the air out of Great Lakes Naval Training Center. His partner, Russ Quint was flying second seat. They were headed east and awaited instructions.

John gave them a brief background on the situation, including a description of the van. He shared his speculations about the gang and their possible terrorist activities. "Sounds like you might have a handle on this John," said Todd. "We'll go with your theory until we come up with something better. We'll be flying due east along I-80. That becomes the Ohio turnpike. We will watch the westbound lanes for the van. We will call in the Illinois and Ohio 'smokies' and instruct them to be on the lookout, but do not intercept until further instructions. Russ suggests we do ground alerts on the connecting Ohio and Illinois interstates as well." John shared his ideas on the possible routes with the chopper crew. Everyone agreed that they were casting a wide net, with only a slim hope of success unless they got a hit from somebody on the ground. They disconnected and John continued heading west.

CHAPTER 33

"There's a rest stop," said Mitch. "Pull into that one. My tonsils are beginning to float."

"I'll need my purse when we go in," said Karen. She was prepared to say that she needed her tampons if they objected, but Mitch handed it back to her. He told her Bolo would wait at the door of the ladies' room, and not to take too long.

The parking area was nearly empty when they went in. Karen could not spot an attendant in the lobby, so she lost hope of trying to get somebody's attention that way. As soon as she cleared the doorway, with Bolo stationed just outside, she hurried into a stall and had one of the quickest pees in recent memory. There were times in the hospital where she had to hurry, so this was not new to her. There was nobody else in the ladies' room, so she quickly went to the mirrors and took out her lipstick. She had already thought of what she would write on the mirror, so it didn't take long. When she went out, Mitch was just joining Bolo on guard duty.

As Bolo left for the men's room, Mitch escorted Karen back to the van. "Cou dn't we get some soft drinks from those machines?" asked Karen.

"Bolo will bring something when he gets back," said Mitch. He took Karen to her side door and had her get in. He told her to check on Dinny while he watched.

Karen couldn't see much different about Dinny. She asked Mitch to hand her the bug-out-bag, but he said to tell him what she needed from it. When she used her stethoscope on

Dinny's chest, he suddenly set bolt-upright and had a dazed look on his face. "Where am I?" he asked.

"We're on the road Dinny," answered Mitch. "You've been out of it for a while. You missed a whole state."

Bolo came back to the van, and true to Mitch's prediction he brought several bottles of water and soft drinks. He got the survival food from the back of the van and gave a couple of energy bars to Karen. She was hoping Mitch would forget, but he didn't. He put new zip ties on her hands and fastened her again to the seat back. He then got in the driver's seat and pulled out of the rest stop just as a beige Buick entered the handicap parking spot beside them. It was an elderly couple. The lady was driving. She looked over at the van and smiled at them as they left. Karen's hopes were dashed. She had been wishing for a bus load of Army Rangers in full battle gear. In her wish John was leading them to her rescue. The elderly lady would have to do. Karen hoped she would respond to the message.

CHAPTER 34

Mrs. Marie Wetsome looked over at her husband Willard and said, "I wonder if that was one of those church vans. They often drive those long passenger vans so they can haul their youth groups."

"Nah," said Willard. "Did you see that scruffy one in the passenger seat. He didn't look like a church person to me. The one behind him was even worse. He looked like a wild man. Get my walker. I have to pee."

Marie had helped Willard to the men's room door. He was able to navigate on his own from there. Travel was a real chore for Marie with having to deal with Willard's difficulties. She went into the ladies' room and went to a stall. She didn't really have to go yet, but Wilard's bathroom needs superseded her own. She did her thing, however meager. When she went to the sink and looked in the mirror, she saw Karen's message written in lipstick. It read:

HELP--KIDNAPPED--IN LONG WH. VAN

Call CAPT OSMOND   724-547-5555

Marie didn't panic when she read the message. There was no one else in the room, and when they came in there were no cars in the rest area that she noticed, other than that long white van. She hurried out to get Willard.

Her husband had worked for several years as the local police dispatcher in their hometown in eastern Pennsylvania. He may have been slipping physically, but his mind was still sharp. Marie had Willard follow her into the ladies' room to read the message. "It may be real, or it may be a prank. Let me call the number. If it's a prank and they hear a man's voice they will probably hang up." Marie gave her phone to Willard as they walked out of the room to a bench in the lobby. They dialed the number from the message.

When Karen wrote the message, she didn't remember John's number, and she no longer had her phone, so she wrote Kurt's number on the mirror. If the message got to the farm, it would work.

Kurt answered his phone and the caller asked if he was Captain Osmond? Kurt thought for an instant and said, "He's not here right now, this is Kurt. May I help you?"

Willard hesitated, then he asked, "Kurt do you know anything about a long white van?"

Jose' was still at the house finishing up his questioning. Kurt motioned him quickly to the phone and held it so he could listen in. "Yes," he said. "I know of a van like you described. It was involved in the kidnapping of my sister."

"Then the message my wife found may be true," said Willard. "It was written on a mirror in lipstick in the ladies' room at a rest stop along the interstate. It said to call Captain Osmond."

"What else did the message say?" asked Kurt. "We've been praying for some help in finding my sister. John Osmond is on the road right now trying to pick up their trail."

Willard read the rest of what Karen had written. Kurt then explained that the police were still at the house where the crime took place, and he asked that Willard speak to

Detective Cantina. As soon as Jose' was on the line, Willard gave him a concise location of the rest area, the approximate time the white van left the parking lot, a general description of two of the passengers in the van, the direction the van was headed, as well as answered questions identifying himself and Marie. All this he volunteered. Then he told Jose' he was an experienced police dispatcher.

Jose' asked the couple to remain at the rest area and meet with a local team of police investigators. He got Willard's number and assured him he would call back with an e.t.a. for the locals. He thanked Willard for knowing his job so well.

Willard was elated. This is the most excitement he has had in his life since he retired. Except for Marie, of course! They sat on their bench holding hands, and anxiously awaiting the next chapter in their adventure. Just wait till they told their son-in-law this story. It would top some of the tall tales he told them.

Jose' switched to his phone to make the necessary calls, while Kurt called John to give him the good news. Karen had come through. Kurt borrowed Jose's note pad with the pertinent location and time details. He passed that all on to John, who promptly disconnected to relay it on to Todd in the chopper. While they talked Russ was calculating the approximate time to intercept the van.

When Todd disconnected, he called the local state police and gave them the rest stop location and the approximate current location of the van. He directed them to try and get an unmarked patrol car in place at a safe distance behind the van once it was located. They would then choose a method and a place of intercept as the situation dictated. He asked that they keep marked patrol cars well back from the target vehicle, in order to keep from spooking them. From here on, Karen's safety would dictate every aspect of the plan.

CHAPTER 35

Mitch didn't waste any time getting back onto the highway. For the first few miles they were all occupied with their gourmet meal of survival food. Karen ate one of the energy bars and drank a little water. She would have liked more, but she squirreled away the second energy bar for her uncertain future. With her demanding hospital work she sometimes missed meals, so this wouldn't be difficult for her.

"Who's she?" asked Dinny as he pointed in Karen's direction. "Where are the other guys?" he asked before Mitch could answer the first question.

"That's Karen. She's your nurse." said Mitch. "Be nice to her Dinny. She helped you get through a bad time. You probably have the virus, and you were in a bad way with it. As far as the *Ruskies* go, they're gone. We don't need them any longer anyways."

Dinny thought for a moment, then said "Good riddance to them. I didn't much like them." Then he looked over at Karen and said, "Good trade Mitch. I'll take her any day over them."

Mitch pondered this situation while he drove on. They had needed the Russians at the Capitol. They were former circus performers in their old lives. Bones and Oreo had climbed up that wall like monkeys. Once the balcony windows were smashed out, they were in. Tats was a strongman in the circus. He plowed forward like a tank, scattering any resistance. This allowed him and Bolo to easily negotiate the stairs and doorways. Once they were all inside, they carried out their prescribed duties before the security forces could respond in enough numbers to end their rampage.

One of the big mysteries was, "How did Dinny get the virus?" He had stayed with the van. His job was to collect them when it was over and get them through the D.C. crowds. "It must have been from those girls they were with the night before it all went down," thought Mitch. "They say it can be hard to detect where it comes from."

They had listened to the radio on the first leg of their journey. They all laughed at how the reporters were grasping at theories for what had brought it on. Some of them were starting to blame it all on Trump, as they always eventually did.

Mitch's thoughts were interrupted by Dinny who stated, "I need to take a leak."

"Why didn't you do that back at the rest area?" said Mitch. "It'll be a long time till we come to another one."

"I didn't need to then", said Dinny. "Now I need to. I haven't been doing so well lately, you know."

Mitch saw an overpass ahead and the pulled out of the traffic lane underneath the bridge. "Do your thing Dinny," he said. He saw Dinny looking at Karen then he added, "Don't worry about her. She's a nurse. They see it all. She won't be impressed by your meager offering." Both Mitch and Bolo laughed at that, while Dinny stepped out, turned his back and took care of business.

When Dinny got back in, Mitch continued down the highway. Karen asked for a towelette from her bag for Dinny. They all kind of looked at her. She explained the need for extra precautions that included washing the hands when dealing with the virus. It might help keep the rest of them from getting it. She also asked for a mask for Dinny. They should all be wearing them, but especially him. They got sobering looks on their faces, and the requested items were handed back.

CHAPTER 36

Todd and Russ were moving along on their search route. One of the difficulties for them was visibility. The sky was clear, and starlit which helped a little, but it was nighttime. They had to fly at a low altitude in order to be able to differentiate the vehicles. The white color of the van would help, and the extra length would also help. Unfortunately, traffic was light, so they did not often have the advantage of headlights illuminating the back of a vehicle.

Luck was on their side. The state police came through. They had spotted the van. They got close enough initially to get the license plate number. The Michigan plate was found to be registered to a van from Ann Arbor. It had not been reported stolen, so it must have been switched from a similar style vehicle. Often it took the victim of the theft several months to detect it. Once the police determined that this was the kidnappers' van, they dropped back to a safe distance to avoid detection.

Having identified the target vehicle, Todd was able to keep out of range until the time he would be needed for a possible intervention. He called John to bring him up to date on the present location and Russ did some calculating to estimate drive times to the upcoming rest areas. The law enforcement people agreed that the best place to intervene would be at a rest area. This was especially so at night when traffic was light. It was hoped that fewer civilians would be in the rest areas then also.

CHAPTER 37

When John learned about Karen's message at the rest area, he had mixed feelings. Mainly, he was happy that Karen had been able to get a message out that solved the dilemma of which route the kidnappers had taken. But John was unhappy with himself. He had missed that call, and it was now going to be tough for him to catch up to them. What he did not figure was that the I-70 route was through a mountainous part of West Virginia before entering Ohio. This ate up some time that was not evident on his map. He had not had the time to play with the GPS to help calculate the timely routes. He had resorted to a quick look at a paper map. That had cost him. But the part that bothered him most was that he had missed on the 'intuition' call big time. Now he had a lot of lost time to make up. He had been running almost constantly with the dashboard emergency light Kurt had given him. So far that had worked favorably. Todd must have told the troopers to let him go through, because he had so far seen three of them set up for speeders.

John was on I-77 travelling north toward Akron when he got the call from Todd that the van had been spotted. Based on Russ's calculations, by the time he got there the van would be well past the point where I-77 intersected with I-80. In addition to that, he would need gas soon. The big hemi had been burning fuel more quickly at the speed he had been driving.

John spotted the high, lighted sign of a truck stop. It was relatively close to the highway. He was glad he had decided to keep his credit card. When things got tight, he almost switched over to all cash for paying his bills. That would really have slowed him at the fuel stop.

It seemed to take forever to narrow the gap between John and the kidnap vehicle. He called Todd a couple of times to double check that he was figuring properly. He was. He kept forging ahead. He hadn't been consuming much liquid, but now he drank a can of *Red Bull*. That would help keep him awake. The interstate driving was taking its toll on him.

CHAPTER 38

Karen had been drifting off to sleep, even in her uncomfortable position of sitting with her hands tied in front of her. Bolo was also nodding off on occasion. Mitch seemed to be wide awake and so did Dinny, who probably didn't need any more sleep with what he's recently had.

Suddenly, Mitch took an off ramp and pulled into a service plaza. He pulled up to the pumps and got out to pump the gas. He told Bolo to go in and get some hot dogs for everyone. The survival food didn't sustain him very long either.

Karen asked to use the rest room while they were stopped. Mitch refused her. "I don't like the looks of this place," he said. What he really meant was that it was too populated, and she would have too much of a chance to escape.

Nobody noticed the unmarked car that pulled into a parking space remote from where the van was fueling. The troopers only watched. This was not a good spot to intervene. That meant it would be a lot more miles of tailing at a distance before they would have to stop again. They called Todd and said they were taking a rest room break, and that he should keep an eye on the target until they could catch up.

Todd held steady on course until the police car was in place behind the target. While he was waiting on them, he called John to alert him about the stop. This should allow him to make up some time and to cut the interim distance considerably. When the smokies had things covered, Todd told them he had to find some fuel soon. "There's an airport near Sandusky where I can get it topped off. I'll get back to you on the flip side," said Todd.

CHAPTER 39

John was feeling much better about his chances of catching up to them since he got the call from Todd. By his present calculation he was about thirty miles behind them. With his speed, he would be able to catch them soon. He could see the first hint of daylight in his rearview mirror. It would become a different game then. The police would have to maintain a greater separation distance in order to keep from being spotted.

John wanted to rush right in and rescue Karen. He realized that the feelings he had developed for her since they met were causing this departure from his normal laser-like concentration. He would have to be exceptionally careful when the rescue confrontation came.

John continued at his high rate of speed. He had overcome his drowsiness when he got closer to his quarry. When he got the call that the van was exiting to a rest area, he began to prepare himself for what was to come, the confrontation.

CHAPTER 40

When they saw the sign that a rest area was ahead, they were all ready for one this time. Mitch laid out the rules for how they would proceed. Dinny would stay with the van while the others entered the building. As before, Bolo would station himself outside the ladies' room while Karen went in. When she came out, Bolo and Mitch would trade places and Karen would accompany Mitch back to the van. Dinny would then take his turn inside.

Mitch was pleased to find the rest area sparsely populated. This was probably due to the time of day it was. The sun was just beginning to give them daylight. Travelers were out of their beds and on the road. Most people who stopped were doing so only to get rid of the effect of that first cup of coffee. There were some big rigs parked in their separate area, but most of the drivers would still be in their sleeper cabs.

Mitch had secured Karen in her zip ties, Bolo had returned, and when Dinny got in they backed out of their parking space and headed for the exit road.

"What the hell is this!" exclaimed Mitch. Out their front window they could see a helicopter touching down on the ramp that pointed back to the highway. It was blocking their way.

Mitch instinctively looked in his rearview mirror. He saw the police car squealing out of its parking place and activating its flashing red light. "Cops!" he said. "Dinny, hand Bolo a shotgun."

Dinny reached behind his seat and grabbed a 12-gauge riot gun with its shortened barrel. He passed that up to Bolo while Mitch was roaring toward the helicopter. When he was about three car lengths away from it, he veered left toward the grassy area and slammed on his brakes. "Take out his rotor," said Mitch as Bolo bailed out and readied himself behind his open door.

Todd and Russ saw the van heading for them at high speed and decided to take up positions on either side of the chopper. They were partway out when Bolo opened fire with the shotgun. It was loaded with OO buckshot. Bolo fired three shots at the main rotor. That means the twenty-seven pellets were creating a pattern of saturation that was highly effective on the machine. Red hydraulic fluid was spewing out and down over the glass canopy and the two crewmen. Bolo jumped back into his seat as Mitch continued his path through the grassy area into the part of the rest area where the big rigs were parked. Truckers don't waste much space in those areas. They generally park relatively closely together. Mitch saw a truck that was just pulling out onto the combination access/exit road. Mitch laid onto his horn as he created a pathway between that truck and the next one. It caused the truck driver to swerve to the left to avoid crushing the van. As a result, the trucker ran into the cab of a nice new shiny Peterbilt that was parallel parked on the other side. The van made it through untouched. Mitch gunned it and they exited the rest area via the truck exit.

The unmarked car was close behind the van but could not make it through the gap.

John was just slowing and entering the ramp leading to the rest area when he spotted the helicopter touching down. Then the police car backed out to go in pursuit of the van. John made a quick decision to stop along side of the entrance road where he could see the action.

It didn't take long to see it all. When he saw the police car stuck among the trucks, he decided to change direction and swing back onto the highway. He gave it the gas and followed the van. There wasn't much traffic yet, so John made his call to Todd to see how they were doing.

"The shooter knew what he was doing", said Todd. "He took out our hydraulics. We won't be flying until that is repaired. I called in some more smokies from the Sandusky area. They will saturate Route 80 in the surrounding area. We'll get them John."

When he disconnected, Todd called his home base about getting a replacement sent out to him. They could do it, but the time would be prohibitive. He had them check on the availability of a civilian chopper in the nearby area. This would take time too.

CHAPTER 41

John was experiencing a bout of frustration. He was so close that he could almost taste victory. He would have Karen back in his life, and his thoughts of late had been to make her a part of his life. He now realized that he was dealing with a very smart adversary. In his deployments he had sometimes encountered an enemy that had what he described as a natural survival instinct. In America that was not as usual. He had been caught off guard by the one Karen said was called "Mitch." According to her, he was the only one who displayed any measure of intelligence. He had quickly and precisely reacted to the trap he suddenly found himself in. The one escape route available to him was a long shot, but he made it work. John vowed to make sure that didn't happen again.

The van suddenly exited the toll road and blew through the stop sign at the end of the ramp. It turned left onto state Route 4 south. John could see why Mitch chose to do this. Staying on the toll road would allow the state troopers to block him in with another pincer-movement at a location of their choosing.

Driving a little slower than Mitch, John followed him off the toll road and into the relatively sparse traffic of Route 4. Mitch had slowed his speed to keep with the traffic flow. This state route was a very straight road. John could keep the van in sight from a long distance, even with some small amount of traffic in between. This worked to his advantage, as he didn't want Mitch to know he was being followed.

John had expanded the view in the GPS screen to maximum. He could try to predict where Mitch might again change course. The next change came rather quickly and was a bit of a surprise to John. Mitch turned right onto US Route 20. The next town on the screen was "Bellevue." It was only two miles from the turn. As Mitch approached the town, he slowed periodically as if he were looking for something. He must have found it because the van turned in to a Dodge/Chrysler dealership that fronted US Route 20. John could see them driving slowly down one of the rows of used cars as he passed. He went down the road a little and turned around.

As John approached the car dealership, he slowed and could see the van had stopped between two rows of cars. John found an empty space in the inner facing end lot. He pulled in there and crouched down to watch what they were up to.

A skinny guy had the door open to what looked like a burgundy Chrysler Pacifica. They were switching cars. Their good fortune was that it was early Saturday morning. The dealership was still closed, and their risk was minimal. They popped the hatch and opened the other doors. The other two guys got out. A bald guy was probably "Bolo", and that left the driver, probably Mitch. The tailgate of the van was adjacent to the back hatch of the Pacifica. They quickly transferred their cargo into the new ride. The skinny guy removed the license plate from the van and put it on the Pacifica. They moved several things through the side doors into the side openings of the replacement. The last thing they moved was Karen.

Mitch had Karen get into the seat behind the driver and was bending into the door opening doing something. He was probably securing her in place. It suddenly came to John that the thin guy was probably dumb, and he was skinny. Therefore, the gang called him

"Dinny." Karen had said the sick guy was called Dinny. It all made sense now, in a perverse sort of way.

They seemed to have finished the switch. Mitch had a tool in his hand as he got into the driver's seat of the Pacifica. In only a few seconds he had the engine running and was backing out of the parking space. It was easy to see what college these three attended.

Mitch pulled onto the highway with Dinny following in the van. John was crouched down in his seat as they drove past him, continuing in the same direction. He pulled out into the traffic lane at a comfortable distance behind them.

CHAPTER 42

The kidnappers drove into the center of town and turned left onto state Route 13 south. John was keeping well back going through town and made the turn cautiously in case he would come up on them too fast. He saw them well ahead and continued to maintain a good distance behind. A short distance out of town they turned onto a secondary road. There was a posted sign that read "Flat Rock, Seneca Caverns." They passed a couple intersections along that road before making a left turn onto a dead-end road. "What do I do now?" thought John. H s instincts told him they were probably looking for a place to ditch the van. He decided to gamble on that and avoided following them onto that road. Instead, he turned and went back to Route 18 and turned to continue going south. His GPS map showed that route intersecting with another state route before a heavier travelled US Route 224. He decided to turn at the first intersection he came to and turn his car to point back toward Route 18. If he guessed wrong, he would have to race back toward Bellevue and turn left onto US 20.

He was pulled off the road watching for the Pacifica to pass by in front of him on Route 18. It seemed to take an eternity, but it finally did. The van was no longer following. "Way to go John. You got that one right!" he thought.

When they came to the town of Republic, the Pacifica pulled into a convenience store and up to the pumps. The stolen car probably didn't have much gas in the tank. John was able to pull off behind some parked cars this time to keep from having to drive past them.

As the stolen car was being gassed, John took advantage of the time to call the state police. Things had been moving so quickly that he had not been able to give them much information about the recent events. He connected with trooper Cooper, the same one that was stuck among the trucks at the rest area. He was pleased to hear from John. They had not been successful so far in catching anyone in their expanded net. John told him his present location and what he guessed the kidnappers would do when they came to US 224. He also told them about the stolen car and gave the best description of it. He still had not been able to get close enough to get the license plate number. He told them where to find the white van.

Trooper Cooper said they would be converging on the location in Republic from various directions. John hoped they could get the net in place before the Pacifica could slip through.

Shortly after the fuel stop, the kidnappers took a right turn. When John got to it, he found that Route 18 bent in a westerly direction. They were headed toward the town of Tiffin. John phoned the police again and gave them the updated route. After they get through this John would have to talk to Karen about having a police radio installed in her car. It would make things a lot easier.

They were staying on Route 18 through Tiffin and toward Fostoria. John could remember his grandmother raving about her Fostoria glassware. Hopefully, he could make a nostalgia trip through this country after this was all over.

In Fostoria, the Pacifica turned right on US 23 north. When they cleared the congestion of the city, they speeded up considerably.

CHAPTER 43

Mitch constantly watched his rearview mirror, given his current circumstances. The time when he pulled out of the convenience store in Republic, he noticed a car pulling out of a parking spot that was the same general color and shape of Karen's car. He wasn't paranoid about it then, but the car made the turn to stay on Route 18 in Republic and then again in Tiffin. When he got to Fostoria the car was still well back in the distance, but still behind him.

Now he was starting to get a little concerned. "If he follows me onto US 23, I'll try to lose him," he thought. When he saw that the blue car was still back there following at the same interval, he put the pedal to the metal. The speed-limit was 70 mph on this road, so Mitch took it up to 85. He passed a couple of cars, but he could still see the blue car back there behind them, and at about the same distance away from him. He held to that speed for about a mile, in which the blue car passed the two cars in between them. He was keeping up.

Mitch dropped his speed back to 65 mph. The blue car kept the same interval, well back from him. He was being followed.

CHAPTER 44

When John noticed the Pacifica picking up speed, he first thought it was because of the higher posted speed limit. But soon their speed increased to 85 mph. John had to pass a couple of cars to keep from losing them. He tried to keep them in sight, but it was becoming increasingly difficult. He really missed having the chopper in the air to help with the surveillance.

They changed speed again. This time they reduced it to 65 mph. Now John had to try to keep a safe distance behind. He was suspicious that he may have been made. The erratic driving was not the norm for Mitch. John called Trooper Cooper to give him a position report. He also told him about the erratic speed. The trooper agreed that the surveillance had been compromised. He suggested getting to a position a normal length behind the Pacifica and staying there. It seemed like they were headed for Toledo. If the tail had been spotted, it would be much easier to lose him when they got into city traffic if he were too far back. US 23 was a straight shot toward Toledo. It took a jog to the left and ran in conjunction with US 20 for about 3 miles to an intersection with state Route 420 north. This juncture would be a critical point in the surveillance, as 420 is a short connecting road to the Route I-80 toll road and, also to Route I-280 north. The latter serves Toledo and some suburbs before joining I-75 into Michigan.

The law enforcement people had some discussion about this and decided that the Route 420 connecting road would be the best opportunity for an intervention. It is a short link, only about two miles long, and is limited access. They would be set up along that route and would block the northern end.

In the event the kidnappers stayed on Route I-20/23 instead of taking the link road, it would be back to the drawing board, because they would be headed straight for downtown Toledo.

John followed the plan and tucked himself in about four car-lengths behind the Pacifica. He noticed what was probably an unmarked car join behind him.

CHAPTER 45

John took advantage of a little free time to call the farm. Kurt was out doing morning chores, so Martha took the call. She was pleased to hear from John, but he could hear the anxiety in her voice. He told her where they were and gave her a brief outline of what had taken place since his last call. He didn't go into a lot of detail about the events at the rest stop, for fear of worrying Martha about the potential danger of a confrontation. She seemed pleased about Karen's ingenuity in leaving the lipstick message. John could only imagine the inner turmoil she suffered. She was fortunate to have the farm work to keep herself occupied, and to have Kurt to lean on.

As the three-car caravan approached the intersection of Route 420 John waited tensely for the lead car to take the exit ramp in the right lane. It didn't happen. They stayed on US 23 and were now about ten miles out of Toledo. About two miles into that route change, John got a call from Todd Farley, of all people. He thought Todd and Russ were out of the picture. In his former life, Russ had been a helicopter mechanic. He called around and located a truck shop that could make up the necessary hydraulic hoses. They got road service to the rest area. After the damaged hoses and fluid were replaced, they were in the air. They had confirmed John's location with the state police and had just had a visual on him.

The alternative for Todd and Russ would have taken too much time. They could probably have located a civilian chopper somewhere in the area but that did not always work out. For another military bird, they would have to wait a longer time to get back into the mission. It could be too late to matter.

John was thrilled to have his "eyes in the air" back in service. In the city they would be invaluable. Surface-only surveillance is not usually as successful when buildings block the peripherals.

CHAPTER 46

Mitch was born and raised in Toledo. It was an old city with old, winding traffic patterns. As the expression goes, "The guy who laid out the streets must have been following a cow." It was easy to find yourself in the wrong lane when you wanted to make a turn. For Mitch it was easy. He would give his "tail" a driving lesson today.

Mitch met Bolo when they were both teenagers. They were from different parts of the city and were in different "gangs." Their gangs weren't rivals, mainly because they were small. They joined together whenever necessary as a protection from one large rival gang. As they grew and were successful, they ventured into Detroit. Through time they got to know the streets there. There was a little more danger, but the rewards were greater.

Detroit is where they met the Boss. They didn't know his name, but they knew he controlled the criminal activities not only in Detroit, but also in several surrounding cities. He drove a nice car and wore expensive clothes. He never got his own hands dirty by directly participating in illegal activities. He had a piece of the action, as the saying goes. For most of the past year they had enjoyed what could be almost called a vacation. Their job was political unrest. They were able to do this work with almost no restrictions as to details. "Smash and Grab" was their specialty. They got paid for their actions, and any loot they were able to fence paid a direct profit to them with only a small tribute to the Boss. Payment was always in cash.

Law enforcement was weak in the cities where they plied their trade. City officials had instructed the police to operate with "mittens" on. They carried riot gear, shields and self-defense sprays, but they rarely used them. They might as well have left their sidearms at home, for they only drew their weapons whenever deadly force was used against them. Bicycles and portable barriers were the tools of crowd control. For Mitch's gang this work environment was the "stuff of dreams." Oft times the police stood back and watched while the terrorists destroyed their cities.

With the rules of the game being established as they were, the Boss instructed the gang members under his control not to use deadly force. Guns and knives were not allowed, although some carried them concealed. They tended to push the envelope though. Lasers were sometimes shined in the officers' eyes. Openly pushing, shoving and spitting were employed, usually without resistance.

The Capitol job had several challenges. It took place in daylight, where most of their work was done at night. They had to appear to be a part of the peaceful rally that was forming outside the Capitol. The crowd was enormous, the largest they had ever encountered. Access required some unique skills. It took some special athletic ability to be able to climb the exterior walls under the balconies.

Breaching the Capitol was supposed to have the appearance of being a spontaneous action of fervent members of the rally crowd. The fact that some high levels of skill were required, and a few people went above and beyond conceivable actions of protest caused general disbelief. One lucky rioter was able to steal the Speaker's laptop.

Was it good enough? Only time would tell. What would follow would be political rhetoric and a news media saturation of the story. The fact that several people died that day during the event will foreshadow the expected results.

Mitch knew that he and Bolo had played their parts cleanly and Dinny was not in the action. He was with the van. What he worried about was the Russians. He didn't know them. They had been foisted upon him for this mission by the Boss. Bones and Oreo had climbed the wall and entered a different area. Mitch didn't see what all they did after they were inside. Tats was the main concern. He was a "weapon" himself. His size and his physical dominance meant he could cause serious harm. Unless he had a measure of self-control that Mitch had yet to see, Tats could be a problem. Mitch had lost track of him for quite a while after they breached the front doors.

Given the uncertainty of the performance of all the gang members, Mitch felt the best solution was to get out of town.

CHAPTER 47

Mitch had just committed to stay on US 23 instead of heading directly north on the east side of Toledo. This choice of route would give him the opportunity to lose his "tail." He thought through his planned route. It would get him to a large warehouse complex where he would have a surprise in store for his followers.

Mitch had called the Boss when he knew for sure he had company behind him. That gave him time for the set-up in the warehouse complex. He had never tested his relationship with the Boss until now. He didn't know what the reaction to his request would be. The man would either be willing to help, or he would go ballistic and tell Mitch to solve his own problems. He would probably be concerned that Mitch would lead the law to their lair. That could prove to be a disaster for all of them.

He was surprised when the Boss reacted mildly. He hesitated for a bit, but then came up with a plan to solve the problem.

The warehouse complex had an entry street that passed between two long rows of similarly styled buildings. They were two-stories high with a large overhead door centered in the lower end-wall of the buildings. The upper level had a single double-hung window to the right and to the left of the door. There was a man-door to the left of the overhead door.

Mitch travelled at a normal rate of speed until he turned into the center street of the complex. Then he gunned it! He needed to get beyond an open overhead door in the fourth building on the left. He needed to do that as quickly as possible.

CHAPTER 48

John was expecting something to happen soon. Mitch had been driving like there was not a problem in the world, and this was not natural given his current location. He got Todd on the phone and put him on the alert for anything unusual.

He was still on with Todd when Mitch made a left turn and suddenly hit the gas. He was hightailing it between two rows of warehouses as if he were trying to lose John. Todd saw the move and was on the alert.

John increased his speed, but with caution. He didn't know what Mitch had in mind, but he didn't want to fall into a trap of some sort. When John reached the second building, he saw it. The overhead door to the fourth building was up and a large van style trailer was being backed out to block the street. Mitch was making a run for it.

"Make a left between building three and four. At the end of the building, turn right and follow that street," said Todd.

John made those two turns and sped along the street that was parallel to the center street of the complex.

"He's turning left at the last building, so hug to the right so he doesn't see you as he passes in front of you," said Todd. "After he passes the end of your street, he has a long block to travel before he chooses which way to go. I'll keep an eye on him, so you can hang back and make sure he doesn't spot you."

John was able to squeeze right and hide behind a dumpster until Mitch passed in front at the end of his street.

"He's making a series of random right and left turns for no apparent reason. This is the part where he will think he has lost you," said Todd. "He obviously knows these streets."

The police car was still following John. He rolled down his window and gave him an OK sign so he would know everything was under control.

"He just passed under US 23 and is rolling north at a more normal speed. He thinks he has lost you. He is on McCord Road, which runs parallel to US 23. There will be some stop signs and traffic lights there, so I will keep you posted. Hang back a safe distance," said Todd. "Oh, by the way, the FBI is now on the case. I'll direct them in if anything breaks. They will be in one of their signature unmarked cars with small hubcaps. That's so nobody can spot them."

CHAPTER 49

Mitch had timed the plan perfectly. The truck had backed out and blocked the road in time to prevent his two-car tail from following. He had sped out of the warehouse complex and into an old section of the city that had lots of narrow and winding streets. Making several evasive moves there, he was sure he was free and clear. Now it was time to get on with business.

Ever the cautious one, Mitch still checked his rearview mirror often as he traversed his planned route to the supply building. Then he called the Boss and reported the success of eliminating the tail. The Boss was in today, and Mitch was told to be prepared to give a report on his mission and the events that followed.

As he drove, he was thinking about what he would say, and what the possible reactions would be. He didn't want to get on the wrong side of the Boss. That could be disastrous.

CHAPTER 50

The building was an older warehouse style edifice located in one of the run-down sections of Toledo. It resembled something one would see in a steel producing city. It had high walls with awning style windows that swung outward to provide ventilation as well as light. An upper level was deeply recessed at the eaves and had nearly solid walls of windows. There were several missing panes of glass in those. What would have originally been large wooden doors at the end walls had long since been replaced with slatted panel steel overhead doors. The building was two hundred feet long and eighty feet wide. This gave the Boss ample room for the various equipment that was used in his various business ventures.

The Boss had acquired the structure for a song. It had sat empty for several years. He had put a new coat of tar on the steel roof but did not do much else to the exterior.

The inside, however, was a different matter. It had an epoxy-coated concrete floor that virtually shined. The open center area was twenty-feet wide and extended the full length of the building. One end had a ground level egress and the other had a loading dock. It was all designed to handle anything from a pickup truck to a tractor/trailer rig. At the end with the dock was a large, fenced parking lot.

There were several man-doors located at the end walls and strategically along the side walls. These were steel construction and had electronic security locks.

On either side of the center aisle were various offices and storage areas. The offices were used as needed by the group leaders of the ventures that operated in the shadows within several states. High up in the center was an office suite occupied by the Boss.

If one ventured into the storage rooms he could find anything from party supplies to gambling devices. There was a room dedicated to supplies for bars and club operations. One recently furnished storage room was dedicated to costumes to be worn by the "rioters" and "protesters" employed in the recent, politicly inspired activities. The office attached to this storage room had a display window like one in a department store. Two mannequins were outfitted in the latest fashion for protesters. They were dressed all in black, including black face masks and boots. Various accessories complemented the outfits that gave them the appearance of battle gear. Mitch had a key to this office.

CHAPTER 51

"What do you think, Bolo?" said Mitch. "Are we in trouble for the way things turned out on this gig? Dinny really threw a monkey-wrench into our plans for the return trip."

"Hey, I couldn't help it!" said Dinny. "I didn't plan to get the virus."

"He wasn't blaming you," said Bolo. "He's just looking at how the Boss might see things." Bolo turned and looked at Dinny, but his eyes shifted in Karen's direction. Dinny got the message.

"Mitch, do you remember Tammy?" said Bolo.

"Yeah," said Mitch. "I was thinking the same thing." Some time ago a woman named "Tammy" was felt to be a risk to the organization. The Boss solved that problem by getting her addicted to drugs. He locked her up for a while in his building. When she was no longer a risk, he put her to work as a dancer in one of his clubs in another city. The inference was that Karen might have that same potential.

They were being careful what they said in front of Karen. From here on, *loose lips could sink some big ships.*

They got quiet as they approached the building. Mitch made the turn to line up to the overhead door and pushed the remote control he held in his hand. The door started to rise.

CHAPTER 52

John sensed that he was approaching something important. Mitch had been driving with a purpose and showing no signs that he was being pursued. John got the shotgun ready in the passenger seat.

"Get closer John," said Todd. "This might be it. He's slowing as if he will turn toward a big building. I'm going to call in the back-up boys."

John hit the gas. In the distance he could see the Pacifica starting to turn left toward a building. As he got nearer, he could see the door rise and the car begin to enter the opening. John tried to time his speed so he would make the turn behind the Pacifica just as it cleared the opening. Mitch would have his eyes forward at that point and would not see his pursuer.

Mitch was fully inside, and the door started to lower as John hit the gas again. He just made it through the opening before the door completed its cycle to the floor. Mitch had pulled forward, in toward the center of the aisle, but John still had to slam on his brakes to keep from hitting the Pacifica.

CHAPTER 53

Mitch was momentarily stunned as he heard the screeching brakes behind him. When he looked in his mirror and saw Karen's blue car, he first looked at Bolo. Bolo was looking back at him with "What do I do?" written on his face.

"Shotgun Dinny," yelled Mitch as he bailed out of the driver's door. Bolo was out equally fast on his side of the car. He took the shotgun from Dinny and directed him toward a forklift that was parked along the right-hand row of storage rooms.

Mitch had flicked open his knife with one hand and opened Karen's door with the other. He quickly cut the ties holding her to the seat back, but not her wrist ties. He pulled her from the car and toward the office door.

When Karen was cut loose and pulled out, she began to resist Mitch's pulling. "Bolo!" yelled Mitch. "Give me a hand with her."

While this was happening, Dinny was running to take cover behind the forklift. He snapped a couple of shots with his '45 toward John, who was on the sheltered side of Karen's car.

John was already out his door and at the ready when Mitch was struggling with Karen. John quickly slid back along the car body to where he could see over the trunk area. He snapped off one "trap style" shot that took Dinny out of the game.

John then repositioned himself behind the trunk area as Bolo slid around the front of the Pacifica to help Mitch with Karen. Bolo took hold of Karen's wrist ties while Mitch got the office door unlocked. When that was done, he fired three shots toward John without any effect other than to destroy the look of Karen's car body. Then the three of them backed through the office door and closed it behind them.

John repositioned himself to the right side of the car and worked his way toward the front. The display window was to the right of the door. There was a straight-backed metal chair beside it. John had an idea. He grabbed the chair and sent it crashing through the display window, mannequins, and back drapery into the room. He quickly positioned himself to the left side of the door. Opening it a crack he saw Bolo raise up from behind a desk and fire a shotgun blast through the back of the display curtain.

John took Bolo out with a double-tap from his Glock-40. That left Mitch.

When Mitch saw Bolo go down, he fired half a dozen shots into the door frame John was hiding behind. Anticipating that response, John had flattened himself on the floor.

Karen jerked on Mitch by way of the wrist ties, even as he got off his last three shots. She followed up with a stomping style kick to the side of Mitch's knee.

Mitch screamed in pain as he clutched at the knee and began to fall forward. Karen spun around enough to bring her elbow down on the back of Mitch's neck. That one put him face-down on the concrete floor.

Karen had let out a little *yelp* when she kicked Mitch. John reacted by getting quickly to his feet and through the doorway. He was there to kick the gun from Mitch's hand as he smashed into the concrete. He quickly got his knife and cut the zip ties from Karen's wrists. They were bleeding from Mitch's pulling.

"My bug-out-bag is between the seats," said Karen. "There are bandages inside."

John grabbed the bag and as he cleaned and bandaged Karen's cuts, he said, "Remind me to never get you mad at me!"

That brought a smile to Karen's face. "I knew I could take him," she said. "This is the first time I have really had the chance."

CHAPTER 54

The Boss had been checking inventory in one of the storage rooms at the opposite end of the building when he was startled to hear gunshots. This was not a usual occurrence in his domain. Such sounds were relegated to the streets. This was his sanctuary.

He was alone today, just putting in time until Mitch arrived. He was anxious to hear what took place that caused him to be delayed in his return. It was not like him. Mitch was one of his most reliable operatives.

The Boss was frozen in place, listening for anything that would explain the two shots he had heard. He certainly didn't expect the shotgun blast he heard next. He went to the door of the storeroom and cautiously peeked out. He could see two vehicles parked inside. Neither was familiar to him. A man was crouched at the door of Mitch's office. A man lay sprawled on the concrete near the forklift. It looked like Dinny. More shots rang out, while he also heard sirens approaching outside.

He waited for his chance, and when the man by the door burst into Mitch's office, the Boss beat a hasty retreat to the back door. He hit the control for the electric gate on the security fence as he exited the building. He had just got out when two state troopers entered at the end where the action was occurring.

The Boss employed a driver for his well-appointed Lincoln limousine. The man also served as a bodyguard. The man had asked for a day off, and it had been granted. "Just my luck," muttered the Boss as he dove into the driver's seat. "I sure could have used Eddie today."

CHAPTER 55

Trooper Cooper and his partner, Trooper Maddie were maintaining a reasonable distance behind John when he raced ahead to clear the descending door. As they approached the door, they heard the first set of shots. They immediately hit their siren and radioed the helicopter. "Shots fired," said Cooper. "Call for backup. We're going in."

By the time they were able to breach the man door, it was over. Karen and John had taken out the last of the opposition. "I'm safe," said Karen as she raised a hand to warn the troopers not to shoot.

As Maddie went to check on the condition of Bolo, Cooper introduced himself and his partner to Karen and John. He did it from a distance, as Karen warned him and Maddie that all of them had been exposed to the virus. Maddie held back on examining Bolo, so Karen went over and did that chore.

John suggested to Cooper that he toss him his cuffs, and he would perform the honors on Mitch. Karen said that Bolo was still alive but had two bullets in him from John's shots. As Maddie called for an ambulance, Karen got her bag of medical gear and proceeded to staunch the flow of blood from Bolo.

When Karen had done what she could for Bolo, John suggested she and Maddie check on Dinny. John had done enough trap and skeet shooting that he could tell when his target was hit by the full load, rather than by one pellet in the perimeter of the pattern. He didn't hold out much hope for Dinny. That feeling was confirmed by Karen when she got to the body. What was probably the result of nine pellets hitting him center mass looked like one big hole. Maddie made another call and asked for the coroner.

When Karen saw Mitch with his hands cuffed behind him, she remembered that he had taken the gun from her purse and put it in his jacket pocket. She told John to check his pockets, and sure enough, there it was. John cleared the gun and placed it on the office desk. He took his weapon from the holster, cleared it and placed it beside Karen's. That left the shotgun and the rifle. He picked up the shotgun, cleared it and placed it on the desk. He told Cooper where the rifle was in Karen's car. He also asked that the three weapons that belonged to Martha and Karen's M & P be returned to them when the investigations were complete.

Trooper Cooper could see that Karen and John were exhausted. He told them to sit on the sofa in Mitch's office while he took down their initial statements. While he did that, Maddie met their backup people, EMT's and the coroner. He had also called in the locals, who would need to be involved in investigating the Boss and his activities in the building.

Karen interrupted Maddie and said, "I need to call my mother back home. She must be worried sick over all of this."

"Sure, go ahead. Take all the time you need," said Maddie. "We'll get back to this when you are finished."

John took out his phone and made the call. "Hello Martha," he said. "There's someone here who wants to talk to you."

Karen had a brief but tearful reunion with her mother and explained that they would be tied up most of the day talking to the law enforcement people. She promised to call again in the evening. She handed the phone back to John and gave him a brief hug before they got back to the interview.

CHAPTER 56

When Todd got the radio message from Cooper, he and Russ saw a man running from the rear of the building and getting into a limo. He squealed out through the gate and onto the street. They took a minute to be sure that backup was on the way to the scene before giving pursuit.

Todd had called in the locals to help with the pursuit of the "runner." They were behind him quickly and were gaining ground. The big limo was not an ideal car for this. The Boss realized this also and made a last-ditch attempt to lose them by driving into the grassy area of a park. It looked like he was attempting a short-cut to an interstate access road. If he could make the interstate, his big engine might make the difference in his run.

Todd saw what he had in mind and went into a dive to cut him off. As the limo made a parallel run along a creek bank, Todd lowered the chopper so that the skids hit the roof of the limo and gave it a healthy bounce. The Boss panicked when this happened and tried to cut the wheels to avoid another hit on his roof. When he did, his rear wheels went over the bank and sent the limo into a twisting turn that culminated with it laying on its side in the creek bed.

Todd had a safe area to land near where the limo's run ended. He was shutting his engine down as the locals arrived, sirens wailing. The Boss was having a bad day all around. He didn't even have a driver's license.

CHAPTER 57

John was trying to keep from nodding off while he and Karen were being interviewed in Mitch's office. He would have probably lost the battle if it hadn't been that Karen was seated right up against him and had her hand in his. The ambulance siren announced its arrival, and that crew came in to get Bolo and Mitch. Karen made sure they observed safety protocols as they performed their duties. They suited up in special jump-suits and gloves. Some wore hoods and face shields in addition to the expected masks.

Before they got far into the interview, John got a call from Todd telling him about the takedown of the Boss. He said the locals were excited about getting that man. He would be giving them more details as things developed.

"That should do it for now," said Cooper. "I can get more detail from the FBI report. They won't let you off so easy since interstate kidnapping laws were violated. They will want to pick your brain for every little detail."

"I don't know about anyone else," said John, "but I need to find a rest room."

"Our crime lab guys have cleared one for our use," said Cooper. "It's just down the hall past the car. Don't mind the fingerprint dust. They should be finished by now."

John was surprised at how many people were busy processing the evidence. Apparently, they were regarding the entire building as part of the crime scene. If he hadn't been under such pressure, he would have liked to see what they were doing. He was moving at a brisk pace when he finally reached the rest room.

When John returned, he noticed Karen looking at him like she was afraid of losing him. He took her hand as they walked to the sofa for another round of questioning, this time by the FBI.

Their interviewers were agents Charles (Chick) Stewell and Connie Faye (Connie) Palmori. They were not your stereotypical FBI agents. They hadn't bought their clothing at the Government Agent Used Clothing Store. Both were dressed fashionably and greeted John and Karen with smiles. They insisted on being called by their nicknames. John threw out all his preconceptions about FBI agents in the first few minutes of dealing with them.

Chick and Connie made the interview easy, and after it was complete it was like the four of them had been friends since high school.

After about an hour had passed, they were joined by Todd and Russ. After introductions were made, John asked Todd, "Where did you park your chopper, Todd? It's a little congested in this neighborhood."

"The Locals are helping with that," said Todd. "We left it right where we landed, in the park. They have a patrol car there keeping an eye on it and the limo. We'll fly out of there when we finish here. If we must stay over, we can find a parking space at the airport. It's beginning to look like that may happen. There are a lot of facets to this case. It might take a couple of days to coordinate it all."

Todd brought the FBI agents up to date as far as the Homeland Security aspects of the case. He gave them a blow-by-blow of what had happened since he came onto the scene. John and Karen were able to interject more information into the overall story as it came together.

John told of how he subdued the three Russians in the barn. He gave them Jose' Cantina's contact information so they could follow up with him on the events that took place at the farm. He also gave them Trooper Weaver's contact information to follow up with the Pennsylvania elements of the "chase" from the farm into Ohio.

Karen told them about the stop the kidnappers made to see Phlegm. She was able to tell them how to find his house, since she knew the local roads that they used to get there. She told them that the three bags in the back of the Pacifica had come from Phlegm's place. She'd heard them mention him as being Bolo's cousin.

Chick commented that Phlegm was an unusual name or nickname. He asked Karen if she knew how to spell it. She gave him the spelling she knew, as a medical term. He suggested that it might be spelled "Flem," as a nickname for someone named "Fleming." He was thinking of the author, Ian Fleming.

"Oh, I hope so," said Karen. "I can't imagine going through life with it spelled the other way. Yuk."

When they were finishing up, Chick brought in a distinguished looking man in a police uniform with gold stars indicating his rank. He introduced Chief Tallman. He was in charge of the local police force. The chief told them what an important day this was for the entire area. The Boss had been operating out of the Toledo area unimpeded for many years. His strategy was to keep his own house clean, while he plied his trade in the surrounding cities and states.

The Boss had been smart enough to separate his headquarters and his records from the nefarious elements of his businesses. "We knew we had a bad apple in our basket, but we couldn't do anything about it," said the Chief. "As long as he didn't break our laws, we couldn't touch him. We didn't have any trouble finding a judge to sign the warrant for us to search this building."

"You're both going to have to quarantine in our city for the next two weeks," said the Chief. "That's the bad news. The good news is that the city will put you up in the Renaissance Toledo Downtown Hotel. It's in a beautiful section of the city, along the Maumee River. In addition to that Karen, your car will be impounded for a short period for our lab boys to go over it. After that it will go to a body shop to have the bullet holes repaired. Then it will be detailed, and the paint restored to original. This will also be done with the complements of the city. We are grateful to both of you for what you have done for us."

CHAPTER 58

When John and Karen were able to leave the crime scene, they were escorted by the Chief to his city owned SUV. They passed on a dinner invitation. They both needed rest more than anything else at this point. John got his suitcase from Karen's car trunk. He also asked for the binoculars he had borrowed from Martha. Everything in the car would be listed in an inventory that he could review once the crime scene techs were finished with their job.

The Chief's car had comfortable second-row seating, unlike the patrol cars that had cages. When Karen and John got into the clean, well-kept vehicle, they were both immediately uncomfortable with their appearance and the condition of their clothing. Karen had not had a change of clothes or a shower since leaving Florida. John had only changed out of his uniform just prior to going to the barn. He was sure he smelled like the barn. Karen didn't look any the worse for wear, but she felt "dirty" from just being around the kidnappers.

"I hope you don't have to have this nice SUV detailed after John and I ride in it," said Karen.

The Chief laughed. "My kids often ride in it after soccer practice," he said. "You're no worse than them."

When they got to the hotel, the Chief took them in and introduced them to the manager. He presented his city credit card and told the manager to charge their suite and whatever they needed to it. He left his business card with John and told him to call his office in the morning after they had breakfast. He promised that there would be no further meetings until at least after lunch.

Karen asked the manager for the hotel concierge. She was introduced to Amy, who was a woman about Karen's age. This made what she was going to ask for easier. Karen explained her predicament and asked if there was a way for her to get some items of clothing. "That won't be a problem if you can wait till morning," said Amy. "I must get dinner for my family after work which is coming up soon. I can shop for you after that and bring everything to you at your room."

Karen gave a list of her sizes and what she needed, along with her credit card. Amy handed the card back and said, "That won't be necessary. I was told to charge it to your room."

CHAPTER 59

John opened the door to their two-room suite and let Karen enter before he lugged his suitcase in and set it down. It was like a world of pressure lifted from him with that one small effort. He looked at Karen and could see the relief in her face as her shoulders slumped.

Neither of them was used to such opulent accommodations. According to the Chief, the city of Toledo is famous for its art glass. That was certainly evident in the spacious hotel lobby, and it had been carried through in the décor of the room. They looked around the inviting living room with its small kitchenette. The city view from the balcony was nothing short of spectacular. The Maumee River at this point was more like a lake. "I could enjoy this view for hours," thought John, "if only I weren't so tired."

Karen looked at each of the two bedrooms and said, "I like this one John, if that's okay with you."

"I could sleep on a rock right now. The other one looks great to me." said John.

"John, I don't have anything to change into after I shower. Is there something in your suitcase I could borrow until Amy gets here with some clothes for me?" said Karen.

John placed the suitcase opened onto the sofa and said, "Help yourself. If you don't mind, I will shower first. I'm afraid to sit on anything here until I do."

"Thanks," said Karen. "I'm sure everything will be too large for me, but I'm willing to sacrifice fit for cleanliness at this point."

John grabbed a clean pair of boxer shorts and an "OD" army tee shirt and headed to the shower.

Karen marveled at how neatly folded everything in the suitcase was. "That's probably his Army training," she thought. She looked through everything but did not find any pajamas. Then she pictured a bunch of GIs in pajamas. It just didn't fit the reality of military life. She finally chose a shirt that would be appropriate to sleep in and another pair of his boxer shorts. She would be just another one of the boys.

John enjoyed that shower more than any he could remember. He not only felt clean but smelled fresh. He realized the need for this improvement in his usual hygiene was because he wanted to make a good impression on Karen. He felt confident as he went back to the living room and to Karen. "Your turn," he said. "That felt great."

Karen gave him an admiring smile as she left for the bathroom with her borrowed outfit. For her the shower washed away much of the "dirty" feeling that kidnap victims have. As she stood under the water, she remembered John coming into the living room in his boxers and tight-fitting tee. She got to see his muscular arms and legs and could imagine how the rest of the package was put together. Allowing herself these thoughts, was therapeutic for her recovery.

When Karen came back to the living room, John was on the sofa looking at the Toledo Visitors Guide. His eyes were beginning to snap shut involuntarily, and he was fighting it. When he looked at Karen, he won the battle with his eyes. "My clothes never looked that good on me," he said as he smiled at Karen.

"I'm beginning to feel human again," said Karen.

Just then the room phone rang. "Not now," thought John as he picked it up.

It was the hotel manager on the line. He told John to turn on the TV, that he and Karen were on the 6 o'clock news.

Karen could hear the manager's voice as John listened to the call, and she immediately turned on the TV and scrolled to the local news channel. They were still talking about the day's events, and especially the arrest of the Boss.

The manager said that the reporters would be chasing after this story, and he suggested that they have a "do not disturb" order placed for their suite. The hotel would not permit visitors without authorization from them. Phone calls for them would be diverted to a hotel associate who would only be authorized to take messages. They could periodically check their messages to decide if they wanted to respond. He said the hotel would do everything possible to protect their privacy.

John thanked him and as he disconnected, he and Karen continued to watch the news story. John had moved the suitcase into his room, so there was room on the sofa for Karen. It was a three-cushion sofa, and John was sitting at one end. Karen chose the middle cushion, next to John. "I hope you don't think I am too forward, John. I just feel safer, somehow when I am close to you," she said.

John gave Karen a serious look as he stretched out his arm and put it around her shoulders. "I'm here for you Karen, whatever it takes. You're going to get through this," he said.

CHAPTER 60

They sat together like that for quite some time. John noticed that Karen had fallen asleep. While she breathed softly in her slumber, John remembered his life as a soldier. From the time he entered his training program he was always too busy to think of a relationship with a woman. Oh sure, there were breaks where his buddies would run to the nearest bar. There were lots of women there, but he wanted a long-term relationship to develop if he was fortunate enough to find the right one. The odds of that happening were slim, so he stuck to his regimen, worked on improving his skills, and put that part of his life on hold till a more opportune time presented itself.

When he did get to a more relaxed duty station in the states, his mother's health began to fail, and he spent his free time with her. For the last couple of years, she was not able to work at her job, so John assigned an 'allotment' to her as a part of his military pay. This supplemented her disability income and gave her a comfortable life. His mother's declining health continued and reached the point that she could not live on her own. That's when things started to affect his military career. The responsibilities he carried as a soldier did not reconcile well with those he had as an only child.

When John left the Army at age 30, he had settled his mother's final expenses and faced his own future. It was with a feeling of pride that he had done right by the woman who had sacrificed everything for him.

As he looked at the beautiful woman asleep in his arms, he wondered if there was a future for them. Would she measure up to the only other woman in his life? Could he be the man she would want in her life?

As the tiredness started to set in, John changed position slightly to relieve a cramp in his arm. They had been sitting that way for over two hours. When he did, Karen stirred and opened her eyes. She looked up at John in her dreamy-eyed state and said, "I think I can sleep now, John. I'd better go to bed."

As she rose, John got up with her. Before Karen went into her room, she turned to John and gave him another one of her signature hugs. This was the best one yet. "While we were riding together on the interstate, in my private thoughts, I wondered what kind of man you were," said Karen. "I am so grateful that you came to my rescue. I tried not to show fear to my captors, but I was really afraid. I can only imagine what was next on their agenda for me."

As she said these words, the tears began to flow. John quietly hugged her in return as they stood together. When she stopped crying, Karen looked up into his face. She reached up and pulled his head down to her. The kiss she gave John was best described as "tender."

"John, I'm not in control of my emotions right now, and you need rest. I'm going to say good night for now. We have a busy day ahead of us tomorrow."

John gave Karen another squeeze, and reluctantly said, "You're right, I'm sure tomorrow will be eventful. I can't even remember the last time I slept. Good night, Karen." He kissed her lightly on the forehead as they stepped apart and went to their separate bedrooms.

CHAPTER 61

John had been this tired in the past. There were times he didn't have a comfortable bed to sleep in, but he was still able to get his needed rest. It was part of his training. He stripped off his tee shirt and stretched out on the king-sized bed. His training failed him this time. He couldn't get Karen out of his mind. He looked at his clock and saw that it was only 8:30. There was still plenty of time for a good night's sleep, so he allowed himself to dream of what life would be like with a woman like this at his side.

Karen turned down the covers on her bed and crawled in. Something didn't feel right. She was used to sleeping in a night shirt. She stepped out and removed John's boxers and got back in. "That's better," she thought.

The kiss had an effect on Karen. She was now wide awake. Did she dare have thoughts like she was having? She hardly knew him. She had read plenty of novels about how the hero rescues the damsel in distress, but now that it had happened to her, she didn't know quite how to react. Nurse's training didn't cover anything like this. She tossed and turned for a while as her thoughts wandered what the future held for her and John. He was headed for New York, and she would be returning to Florida. Could she even think that a relationship was possible in those circumstances? She could easily fall for him, that's for certain.

Karen looked at her clock and saw that it was only 9:15 PM. It had been a very long day, and she was having a difficult time getting to sleep. She became concerned about John. He had to be exhausted. She got out of bed and tip-toed over to the door of his bedroom. He hadn't closed it completely, so she tried to see if he was asleep. She couldn't see in well enough to tell, so she said quietly, "John, are you awake?"

"Yes," he answered. "I can't seem to relax."

Karen pushed the door open and stepped into the room. The lights from Toledo shining into the living room backlit Karen as she stood just inside his room. He noticed right away that she no longer wore his boxers. His long/tall sized tee shirt was the perfect fit for her as a night shirt. It was only just long enough.

"John, I apologize for forgetting my nurse's training. We were taught that a patient is often stressed at having gone through hospital procedures. Maybe a back rub would help you relax. I'm good at it," she said.

"That might be just what I need," said John.

As she walked up to the edge of the bed, John rolled over onto his belly. Karen leaned over and began to give his back muscles a deep massage. Her hands were surprisingly strong. She worked the kinks out of his neck and shoulder muscles. It felt great. As she was working on his lower back muscles, she asked, "How are your legs?"

John quickly offered in a squeaky reply, "They could use it too."

Karen started at his ankles, working the calf muscles first and continuing up to the thighs. The stress melted away.

"That takes care of all my aches and pains except my butt," said John. "All that sitting in the car……." He raised up, and Karen helped him slip out of his boxers. She gave a hard massage to his gluteus maximus as John moaned softly into the pillow.

"If you'll turn over John, I'll do the front of your legs," she said.

John turned over and Karen began to work on the front of his leg muscles, beginning again at the ankles and working up. As she passed his knees, leaning into her work, she was breathing hard, almost panting. It had the same effect on John, and when he could stand no more, he reached out, put his arms around her and pulled her into the bed with him. "You're an excellent nurse," he said. "I think I'm *almost* totally cured."

Karen broke free from his arms for a moment. She raised up and pulled the tee shirt over her head, as she said, "Your shirt is getting to be a little cumbersome, John."

CHAPTER 62

Mitch was banged up badly, but the pain associated with that was the least of his concerns. He knew the Boss was in the building when he pulled in. He was supposed to be there to meet with him. They had talked only a minute before all of this. Mitch hoped he had gotten out of the building before the shooting started, but he didn't know.

He could hear parts of the conversation between Karen and the guy driving the blue car, and bits of the later conversation they had with the police. He hadn't been able to piece enough together to make any sense. His thoughts kept going back to what the guy in Falls Church said about not wanting to be the guy that caused the mission to fail. Mitch knew how the cops could take a thread of evidence and weave it into an entire wardrobe. He would have to be cautious in how he spoke from here forward.

Mitch kept quiet as he was being attended to by the EMT's. He suffered a broken collar bone and a torn lateral collateral ligament. It was hard for him to accept that these injuries were inflicted upon him by a woman, by a woman who was handcuffed! He would never again trust a woman who was bigger than he was.

Before he was loaded into the ambulance, he was approached by two law enforcement people he thought to be detectives. Unfortunately for him, they turned out to be FBI.

"I am Special Agent Stewell," said the male agent, "and this is my partner, Special Agent Palmori. What is your full name, please?"

"My name is Truman Mitchell, but my friends call me Mitch."

Agent Palmori read Mitch his rights and placed him under arrest for the federal crime of kidnapping.

"Do you understand these rights as they have been read to you?" asked Connie.

"Yes."

"Are you willing to answer a few questions to help us establish some background?

"I am willing to answer questions as long as they do not incriminate me in any way. If I feel that line is crossed, the interview will be over, and we can contact my attorney."

"That's fair enough," said Connie. "Let's begin with your home address."

"I live at the Sycamore Apartments on 4th Avenue, number 218."

"How long have you lived at that address?"

"Oh, for about 19 years."

"And before that?"

"I lived at several addresses in Detroit. I was born there."

"What is your occupation, Mr. Mitchell?"

"I am a warehouse manager and bookkeeper."

"Where is the property you manage?"

"There are some properties in Detroit and some in outlying areas."

"What types of properties are these?"

"Some are storage warehouses, some have retail establishments, some are apartment buildings, a variety of things."

"Is this building one of the ones you manage?"

"Let's get away from the properties, shall we? I don't know where we're going here. I may want the attorney before I answer more questions about that subject," said Mitch.

"Okay, tell us who your two companions are and how they came to be with you today."

"The one they took in the ambulance is Robert Ball, nickname 'Bolo'. The other one, over there by the forklift, is Arnold Dinsmore. We call him 'Dinny'. Can you tell me how they are doing?"

"Certainly," said Connie. "Mr. Ball has suffered two gunshot wounds to his torso. He appears to be in serious but stable condition and has been transported to the hospital. Mr. Dinsmore suffered multiple wounds to his torso and unfortunately did not survive." How were they associated with you, Mr. Mitchell?"

"They have both been lifelong friends. They helped me with the properties."

"Can you tell me where they lived?"

"They both lived in the same apartment building as I do. Bolo is in number 114 and Dinny is in number 119."

"Thank you, Mr. Mitchell. That's all the questions I have for you at this time. We'll want to talk with you further once your injuries are taken care of. My partner has some paperwork for you now."

"Mr. Mitchell, I'll make this brief," said Agent Stewell. "This form states that you understand your rights as they have been explained to you. It also states that you are being charged with the crime of kidnapping. I have also included your conditions of cooperating with us in permitting limited questioning prior to contacting your attorney. We need you to sign both copies of the form. We will keep one copy. You can keep the other one to give to your attorney."

Mitch read over the document and hesitated for a moment before asking one question.

"When can I contact my attorney? he asked.

"Anytime you want," answered Stewell. "I see the EMT's are ready to transport you, so I suggest you do it from the hospital. He will want a private conversation with you anyways, and that would be a good place to have it."

Mitch pondered his situation for a couple of minutes. He had probably given more information than he should have, so he decided to clam-up and not ask any more questions. He signed the documents.

As the ambulance pulled out Stewell said, "You timed that perfectly, Connie. He was just about to slam the door on our questioning."

"It was my feminine wiles," said Connie. "He probably likes women who are shorter than he is. I'll go schmooze a judge and get warrants for the three apartments. Why don't you check with the state guys to see how fast we can get a look into that upstairs office in this building. If we move fast, we can get a handle on this before we start tripping over lawyers."

"We're lawyers, Connie," said Chick.

"That's different," she answered. "We're the 'good guys.'"

CHAPTER 63

Chick made his way to the upstairs office. It was fortunate that it was a large room because it was packed with law enforcement people when he got there. He found Todd on the phone, and Russ and a state policeman over near a large safe.

"It's a treasure trove," he answered. "Those locals over there are going through paper files. A lot of it seems to be legitimate, but there are some questionable things too. They found a tie to your boy, 'Mitch' in some of it."

"What's with the safe?" asked Chick.

"Nothing yet. My friend here with the headsets is trying to crack it. It appears to be a tough one."

Suddenly they were all interrupted by the loud wailing of a siren. The safe tech had just started to open the door of the safe when it went off. He jumped up and immediately located the source of the sound. He reached up and pulled the housing off the wall and snipped a wire. The sound stopped.

"Sorry about that, guys," he said. "The door to this room was wired, but the perp left in such a hurry he forgot to re-set it. We missed this one. He must have been paranoid about security to have this second level of protection."

They all heard a siren approaching the outside of the building.

"That's got to be the security company," the tech said.

One of the locals volunteered to go down and tell them it was under control.

With all the commotion Todd had finished his call. He had been talking with Jose' Cantina about the Russians at the farm.

"Jose' says the big one gave his name as 'Ivan Kuznetzov.' If he had been an American, that would be like saying it was 'Joe Smith.' It's probably an alias. His nickname was 'Tats.' He had sleeve tattoos on both arms, was about 6' 5" and went well over 300 lbs. He's the one John told us about who tangled with the bull. Jose' says the bull won. The next guy, the one they called 'Oreo' was small and wiry. He gave his name as Oleg Yermentov. The last one, 'Bones' was named Gregori Kravchenko. He was another small, wiry guy. Jose' will be sending us mug shots to help with further identification."

"Todd, how did it go with the big-shot in the limo?" asked Chick.

"All we got out of him was 'I want my lawyer'. I don't think he realizes how much his employees got him into. I'm guessing that he and Mitch will have the same lawyer. It'll be hard for us to get Mitch to roll over on the big guy that way. Mitch is smart though. Hopefully, he'll realize the only chance he has is to separate himself and try to make a deal with us. Among the bad guys, Mitch has all the cards. He just has to figure that out."

"Connie got names and addresses out of him," said Chick. "She's requesting a search warrant on three apartments. Mitch and his boys will be implicated in not only the kidnapping, but probably a lot we find here. Have you heard anything on the condition of Bolo?"

"He's out of surgery and in recovery. He has a good chance. We should know more in a couple of hours," said Todd.

"I hope he makes it," said Chick. "If Mitch decides to play hardball with us, we can tell him Bolo wants to deal. That will put a little pressure on him from the other direction. John said one thing that has been bothering me though. He told me that Mitch uttered the words 'arm rest' just before he passed out. I asked him if it could have been something else, but he was confident that's what he heard. I've been wracking my brain trying to figure that out. I can come up with two possibilities. One would have him attempting to make a 'dying declaration' if he thought he was checking out. With all the shooting and his blackout level pain it could be that. The pain might also cause him to confuse who he was talking to. He may have been trying to tell one of his henchmen something important that needed to be attended to. In either case 'arm rest' could be important. John has a theory that Mitch may have hidden something in the car and was worried that he did not have enough time to retrieve it when the shootout occurred. I'm going to have our boys go over it in detail when it gets to the impound lot."

"We can kick that around with John when we meet tomorrow," said Todd. "Karen may also have an idea on this."

"Good," said Chick. "Connie may have something for us on the other searches by then."

CHAPTER 64

Karen was awake at 6 AM. Her internal clock rarely failed her and even the crazy events of the past couple of days did not change that. The one thing that was different was that she had a warm body in bed beside her. A wonderful warm body. She was lying on her side facing John, remembering last night and how they eventually fell asleep in each other's arms.

"I wish it could go on like this forever," she thought. She let her mind wander about how life would be like with John. He was still sound asleep, and no wonder. It's amazing what he had gone through since they first met.

"As much as I want to stay here," she thought, "I'd better get up and let him catch up on his sleep." She donned the discarded make-shift night shirt, crept quietly out of the bedroom and pulled the door closed.

The message light was blinking on the phone. It was from Amy, the concierge. She had done the shopping and would bring her purchases to Karen whenever she was ready. Karen called her back.

"Amy. This is Karen Grant. Thank you for the quick service on getting the clothes. If it's convenient you can bring them to me now. Be quiet when you get here. John is still sleeping, and I don't want to wake him."

"I'll just drop off what I have," said Amy. "I can return anything you don't want. We can talk later. I will be here all day."

Karen watched for Amy at the door. She opened it a crack and reached around to get the bags. She thanked Amy and said she would see her later to let her know how everything fit. She felt a little awkward about not inviting her in, but there was no use advertising how she was almost naked.

She took the bags into her bedroom and spread the contents out on the bed. Amy had done a good job. There was a pair of jeans and two different style tops. One was casual and one was more fashionable. Socks, underwear and a belt rounded out the clothing purchases. She couldn't have done a better job herself. There was also a small bag with some basic cosmetics. It looked like Amy might have raided her own home supply and made up a 'care package' for her.

She decided to wait until she got a shower to get dressed in the new clothes. After last night she could use another shower. She thought she would be able to do laundry later in the day and do some of John's clothes as well as her own. She could give him back his boxers, but she planned to keep his t-shirt for a nightshirt. She didn't think he would mind.

She sat down on the sofa and turned on the TV. The local channel still was reporting on the shootout at the warehouse. It probably wouldn't be long before the reporters tracked them down. When the news channel switched from local to national news, they had a story about the US Capitol. Karen was absorbed in what had been discovered following the day of the breach. She had missed nearly all of it other than what was discussed among her coworkers and patients at the hospital before she left. She was anxious to have a conversation with John about his theories. She knew he suspected Mitch's gang's involvement, but she didn't know why. She had ideas of her own that she wanted to share with him.

John's bedroom door opened a little and he peeked out into the living room. Karen saw him and smiled.

"Good morning sleepy head," she said. "I didn't want to wake you since you were sleeping so well."

John came on into the room. He was shirtless but had put on his boxer shorts. He looked at Karen sitting on the sofa and noticed that she was wearing his t-shirt again. It was riding up a little.

"What a way to wake up," thought John. "I could go for this *every* morning."

"It's about 7:30. Do you want to order breakfast yet?" Karen asked. "I need a shower, but we can eat first if you would like."

"Me too," said John, "on the shower, that is. For some reason sleeping wore me out last night. Let's eat first. I need to replenish my energy."

Karen laughed at that as she got up from the sofa and went to the phone. John couldn't help but watch her every move.

She handed John the room-service menu and he told her what he would like. As she stood in the morning sunlight in that t-shirt making the phone call, John was reminded of a little song he once heard:

'Nellie got a brand-new dress. It was so very thin.

When she asked me what I thought of it, I told her with a grin,

"Wait 'till the sun shines, Nellie...."

John's brain tended to work that way.

They looked at each other, somewhat awkwardly after the breakfast was ordered. Everything between them had happened so fast that a natural shyness suddenly had set in.

"I guess we have a lot to talk about, John," said Karen as she shrugged her shoulders.

Then they came together in one of the Grant woman signature hugs. Karen's hug had a different effect on John than Martha's did though.

"I have a plan," said John. "If the person bringing our breakfast is male, I will answer the door. If female, you answer. I'll get some money ready for a tip and watch through the peep hole."

"Good plan John. I can see why you were successful in the military. Plan ahead."

John went for his wallet and got some bills for the tip. He stationed himself at the door.

"Male," he said. "Scoot into your bedroom while I take care of it."

They both thought it was a great breakfast. Of course, part of

it could have been that they were enjoying each other's company.

"I'll shower first John, if that's okay," she said. "It takes the girls a little longer to get made up. I'll do that while you shower."

"Fine with me," said John. "I'll clean up our breakfast and put the cart out into the hall."

John did that, and then hung a 'do not disturb' sign on the door handle.

John stood at the bathroom door and heard the shower running.

"May I come in?" he asked.

"What do you need?" asked Karen.

"Well, I was remembering how great I felt after the back rub I had last night, and I thought I could return the favor and wash your back for you."

"I have always had a little trouble reaching my back to do that properly," she said. "I guess if you promise to do a good job you can come in."

"I promise," said John as he entered the bathroom and stepped out of his boxers.

The shower was plenty big enough for the two of them. Despite that, it seemed to take longer than expected to complete the joint effort. When they finished, they went to their separate bedrooms to get dressed for the upcoming meeting. It was nearly 10 AM.

CHAPTER 65

When John and Karen entered the meeting room, they found several law enforcement people already there and working.

"Well, you two appear to be refreshed," said Chief Tallman. "I hope we gave you enough time to get rested."

"We're good to go," said John. "It's surprising what a good night's sleep will do."

Karen felt herself blush a little. She hoped nobody in the room noticed. At least they didn't laugh and point fingers.

When they were all seated at the table the chief volunteered to act as moderator.

The following were in attendance: the two FBI agents, the two from Homeland Security, and two from the Ohio State Police. The chief represented the local police. He had brought along his secretary to record notes of the meeting. There was also a teleconferencing connection with Jose' Cantina of the Mount Pleasant police and Trooper Weaver of the Pennsylvania State Police.

After introductions were made the chief asked the FBI to go first. Agent Stewell gave the details of the arrest and charges before presenting an outline of the questions and answers from the interview. He also reported on the findings of the crew searching the Chrysler Pacifica and the warehouse building.

In the car they found several weapons that were in addition to the ones used by the shooters.

The Chief asked John and Karen to give background information about how they came to be involved in the case. They told their story from the time they met as travelers along the interstate, about the text message from Kurt to Karen, and about their decision to go quickly to the farm.

John gave the group some information about his experience in the military and how they put that into play when they reached the farm. He explained how he eliminated the three Russian players and secured them in the barn.

Karen told of her experiences when she got to the house, how she dealt with Mitch and the others until the time they took her to the van and basically kidnapped her. She remembered one helpful detail about the money they paid Martha for breakfast. It was all new twenties with consecutive serial numbers.

Chick interrupted and asked Jose' to get those bills from Martha and give her a receipt. They would be important evidence if they matched up with the money they found in the Pacifica.

Karen continued and told of her ordeal being tied in her seat during the trip. She told of being alone long enough at a rest stop to leave the message on the mirror. She also reported about the stop earlier when they met with Phlegm and picked up duffel bags that had some food. The bags appeared to be heavy and probably also contained some of the weapons that appeared later.

Trooper Weaver reported that they had a line on Phlegm. They believed him to be one 'Richard Fleming'. Karen's location information helped them arrive at that reasoning. He was somebody they had long suspected of dealing in illegal firearms. Weaver would coordinate with the FBI on when he should pick him up.

John told of how he borrowed weapons from Martha and of how Kurt helped him get quickly in pursuit of Mitch. That was the time they brought in the local police and consequently also the state police. John told Jose' where to find the Russians. He also established communications with him so he could pass that on to the state police.

Karen passed on what information she could regarding the auto theft and the disposition of the white van. She remembered the name of the dealership. She could also give accurate directions to where they ditched the white van.

Trooper Cooper reported that they had recovered the stolen van which now resided in an impound yard in that area. He also obtained documentation ID on the Pacifica that was stolen to match with the car they now had. The stolen license plate was the one from the van and the previously reported Michigan car.

Karen told of a conversation between Mitch and Bolo concerning a woman named Tammy. It was vague, but Karen believed her to be a previous kidnapping victim. How they resolved their problems regarding her was probably going to be the same solution for Karen.

John told of the ambush they had planned for him earlier at the warehouse complex. Karen filled in what she could of what she guessed was Mitch's plan.

Todd told about the aerial surveillance and how that led to John's breach of the warehouse and the capture of the fleeing limo. He presented some additional detail on what was found in the upper office. The contents of the safe proved to be incriminating for the Boss. There were some files that were obviously blackmail photographs of some prominent people. A large stack of consecutively numbered currencies in hundreds and twenties was recovered. There seemed to be some type of protection racket going on. Collection efforts by 'M' were often mentioned in the records.

Chick reported that Connie had tried to question the Boss that morning. He had lawyered up and wasn't talking. About all they learned was his name, Wade Dilmore. They think his attorney just needed more time to find out what he was involved in. Meanwhile he's cooling his heels in a jail cell. They'll try again this afternoon.

"That seems to have brought us up to date," said the Chief. "Does anybody have more to offer?"

"In that case we'll adjourn and meet again when we get more detail in the case."

CHAPTER 66

Karen and John returned to their suite following the meeting.

"I'm going to do some laundry, John," she said. "I'm anxious to do the clothes I travelled in. I'll feel better when I wash out some of that experience. I'll do yours for you too if you want. I'm not sure I will be able to do them to military specifications, but I'll try."

"I would appreciate it. Laundry is not my favorite thing. I need to call my friend in Jamestown and let him know what happened to me. That will probably take some time."

John had been thinking about whether he really wanted to go to Jamestown. He liked being with Karen a lot. He knew she felt the same way about him. There were some logistical problems to work out, but most relationships had compromises to make. He hoped theirs would be one of the successful ones.

Karen found the hotel guest laundry and set about getting their clothes in the washer. She took advantage of the private time to phone her mother.

"Mom, you'll never guess what I'm doing," said Karen. "No, I'm not having lunch. John and I had a late breakfast. I'm doing laundry. You sound good. How is Kurt?"

"He's back to working his full schedule of chores," said Martha. "He can't go back to driving the bus yet, but the free time allows him to tackle a few things around here that have been piling up. He really misses the kids, but it's still too soon for him to go home. Sheila is holding up well. If you can, give her a call after the kids are in bed. She is anxious to hear from you. How is John?"

"John is great, Mom. I can't tell you how great he is. I really like him. He's talking with his friend in Jamestown that had the job lined up for him. I hope he decides not to take it. Right now, I just can't imagine my life without him in it."

"Well, I only spent minutes with him, but if my impression was accurate, I think you are right. My only advice is for you, for both of you to take it slowly. You both have a lot of life ahead of you. Just make sure your judgment is not clouded by what you went through. I hope you will bring him back to the farm with you so we can all get to know one another. Kurt likes him too."

Karen talked with Martha while she finished the laundry. It was the most they had been able to talk since all this happened to them. When she got back to the suite John had fallen asleep on the sofa. She had just been too hard on him lately. She busied herself folding clothes and doing some ironing. When John was awake, they ordered lunch.

CHAPTER 67

Mitch was sitting on his bed in the county lockup. He was contemplating his options. The charge against him was kidnapping. That alone was serious. There was still the unknown factor of additional charges. The state would certainly charge him with grand theft auto. There would be possible charges for the weapons violations, and any number of possible charges for his actions at the farm.

There was also the matter of his implication in the can of worms that would come out of what they found in the Boss's office. He was the Boss's number one man. The records they found or have yet to find could tie him into enough criminal acts that he would likely never see the light of day. The picture was grim.

His meeting with the Boss's attorney did not inspire confidence. The guy went through the motions of insisting that he be present during any meetings with law enforcement. He was to make no statements to the press.

While in the brief private conversation he had with the attorney, Mitch came to realize that his legal rights and protections were secondary to those of the Boss. This was the Boss's lawyer. That relationship had existed for many years, probably, longer this his own relationship with the Boss. He had little doubt that he would be thrown under the bus before this was all over.

The Boss had been extremely lucky in his criminal career. His reputation was not the best, but he had always expertly dodged all the accusations that came his way. He had entrusted Mitch to help pave the way to that success.

As Mitch reflected on his past, he remembered the many close scrapes he overcame. He had not been arrested since he was a teenager, and the records of those early offenses were probably sealed. In keeping himself clean, he had been the driving force in keeping the Boss clean. Now it appeared he would be the one to cause it all to fail.

"Or would I," thought Mitch. "I'm not the one who got us involved with the heavy hitters. There was no reason to get us involved in politics on a grand scale. We were doing fine in our successful and growing empire. Sure, the money was easy, and the risk was small, until the game got too big. The gigs in the cities were something we could handle. Our past experiences gave us the know-how to pull them off. The US Capitol was too much for us to be able to control. As it turned out, the *virus* was what brought us down."

"I am the link in the chain that leads to the Boss," thought Mitch. "If I were in his shoes, I would make sure that link did not exist."

As his speculations ran deeper, Mitch remembered the answer the Chairman gave him when he posed the question of *what happens if something goes wrong*. His response had been, "I wouldn't want to be the one who caused it." If the connection were made of the Boss's involvement in the riot at the Capitol, again it would be Mitch who would be the important link in that chain of events.

"I've often heard that situations like this caused a knot in the stomach," thought Mitch. "The knot in mine feels like it's made of steel cable."

Just when he thought things couldn't get any worse, Mitch remembered the white van and where he hid the flash drive.

CHAPTER 68

John heard the activity of the room service lunch delivery and awoke from his nap. He found Karen busily setting out the food and humming a tune. It was good to see her improved state. He had been concerned that the stress of her recent traumatic events might linger with her for a much longer time. He had seen friends suffer from PTSD while they were deployed. Some took months to recover. Some were seemingly permanently damaged. This was a strong woman.

"Did you enjoy your nap," she asked. "Lunch is served."

"I must have needed that," said John. "I didn't intend to fall asleep, but I guess I still needed to catch up."

They talked as they enjoyed their lunch. Karen had chosen well from the menu. "I wonder if she can cook," thought John.

"I had a great conversation with Mom while I was waiting for our laundry to dry." Karen said. "She sounded like her old self. Everything is going well at the farm. Kurt seems to be fully recovered now."

"I hope I can meet your family under more normal circumstances," said John. "Things were hectic then. I had to move quickly to catch up with that van. Did your mother ask about me?"

"Yes, she did. We had a nice conversation about you. Mom thinks you're a wonderful guy, having rescued her favorite daughter. I kind of think so too."

They sat quietly for a long time as they finished their meal, each with his own thoughts.

"There's something I should tell you, John," said Karen. "I want you to know that I would not usually jump into bed with a man I only knew for a day. I *needed* you. You helped me come out of the dark place I was in. I must admit though, I also *wanted* you. Had we met under different circumstances I would have suppressed those feelings for a longer time."

"I understand," he said. "I know that most men would be anxious to get to the *sex* as expeditiously as possible, but I have never been that type. I have certainly had the desires, as would any healthy male, but I have tried to look beyond that. I believe that any interpersonal relationship must be workable for *both* parties. No matter what type of transaction it is, each side must be satisfied. That transaction between a man and a woman is the most important one that any of us would make. I could see your need, Karen. I told you I would be there for you, and I'm happy things worked out for us the way they did. If our relationship doesn't go any further, I would understand. I would be disappointed though. I really want to get to know you better."

Karen reached across the table and took hold of John's hand. A couple of tears were running down her cheeks as she said, "I want that too. I want that very much."

They spent the rest of the afternoon talking about any variety of things. It was almost like they were having a cram course in romance. Dinner came and went. They enjoyed another of the hotel's wonderful meals together.

After dinner they turned on the TV for the evening news. The top story was still the Capitol riot. *Finger pointing* was beginning to be the most prominent topic. Journalists today can get away with wild speculations without consequence. Not to worry, for a more outrageous story will take its place soon.

John and Karen watched attentively as each crowd scene appeared on the screen. They thought they may have seen Bones and Oreo climbing the wall up to the balcony, but they were not sure. They were looking at their backs, and the picture was only on for seconds. On another scene, they were sure they saw Tats bullying his way through a barricade and a line of policemen. There was a back view of a man close behind him that could have been Mitch. John made a mental note to tell Todd about this. Homeland security might have access to more film footage that they could look at. It's likely that law enforcement would be interested in the activities of Mitch & Company leading up to when they appeared at the farm.

After the news they watched several of the talking heads to get their versions and embellishments of what *actually* happened. When they had enough of that, they watched a movie. Karen made some popcorn from the hotel's complimentary stock, and they sat on the sofa together. Life was improving for them.

They watched the eleven o'clock news, which turned out to be more of the same except for the weather report. Tomorrow was to be almost *balmy*. They planned to sneak out and go for a walk. They were anxious to experience some of what they could see from their window.

John noticed the message light. "I wonder how long that has been blinking," he said.

When he retrieved the message it said, "Meeting tomorrow at 10 AM. Same location. Same subject. Chick."

They had talked a little more when Karen stood and said, "I think I'll go to bed. I didn't have a nap like some people."

"Me too," said John. He stood and walked up to Karen. He took her in his arms and gave her a serious good-night kiss. He then turned and headed for his room. "10 AM comes quickly,"

John had been in his bed for a while, staring at the ceiling. It had been an eventful day. That had been the norm for him since he met Karen. He was still awake with his thoughts when Karen appeared in his bedroom doorway.

"I gave it a good try," she said. Like someone in the hundred-yard dash, she moved into his bed and latched onto him.

"I never liked my tee shirt this much before," thought John as it crushed up against him.

CHAPTER 69

Mitch looked through the meager possessions he was permitted to have with him in his cell. He found the business card that had been given to him by Agent Stewell of the FBI during their initial meeting. As he toyed with the card, he was going over in his mind the concerns he had about his legal representation. He was all but certain he was going to be the sacrificial lamb that would protect the Boss. It wasn't good that they had the same attorney. If he said he wanted a different lawyer now, it would be suspect in the Boss's eyes. That could be life threatening. Mitch finally decided. He made the phone call.

"This is Agent Stewell. Who's calling, please?"

"This is Truman Mitchell. I've been doing a lot of thinking, and I want to talk to you again, this time without my attorney being present."

"That may not be advisable, Mr. Mitchell. I could get into trouble if we did that."

"I realize that, and I want you to make a document that protects you in having a private meeting with me. I'll sign it. I think what I have to say will be important to both our advantages."

"That should work. Does this afternoon work for you?"

"I think I can work you into my schedule," said Mitch. "If the lawyer calls, I'll tell him I have the 'runs' or something."

"Do you have any problem with me bringing my partner?"

"Not at all," said Mitch. "I'll be here all day. Come any time you like."

They agreed to meet at 2 PM. Mitch felt like a burden was lifted. He was possibly going to have a chance to help his cause.

CHAPTER 70

As per Karen's wishes, she and John got to the meeting early and were waiting when the others arrived. Maybe they would not have to endure the 'all knowing' smiles from them. They probably all suspected the budding romance that was in progress.

The Chief called the meeting to order when everyone was present. All the entities were represented, although a couple of them by only one person rather than two.

"We had our session with Wade Dilmore, aka the Boss," said Chick. "He's trying to sell us a wild story. According to him, Mitchell only *rents* from him. He denies any involvement with Mitchell, Dinsmore or Ball. He claims he only ran from his building when he heard gunfire in the center aisle. He says he feared for his life.

"When we asked him about some of the incriminating things that were found in his office, his lawyer jumped in and declared that anything found there was the result of an illegal search and would be inadmissible," said Connie. "It looks like Dilmore is expecting Mitchell to take the fall for a lot of things. It'll be interesting to see how that plays out."

"What Connie alludes to is that Mitchell has asked for a private meeting with us, without his lawyer being present," said Chick. "I have prepared a waiver for him to sign. We're going to meet with him this afternoon. We believe he will want to deal."

"There's probably some room for a deal, in that no innocent was harmed in the kidnapping effort. How do you feel about that, Karen?" asked Chick.

"You're right that nobody was physically harmed, but I certainly was scared out of my wits at times. At the farm, they were more disruptive than anything else. John punished the Russians already, and our bull, Jake, gave Tats something to remember him by. My wrists are healing nicely from where they tied me. The worst part is that I haven't been able to get past the thoughts of what my future was going to be. I guess if you can strengthen your case in the aggregate, it's alright with me if you make a deal with Mitch."

"That's good, Karen," said Connie. "We'll run any potential deal past you before it is finalized."

"Our lab boys have gone over your car and could not find anything hidden in the arm rests, or anywhere else for that matter," said the Chief. "We've taken it to our contract body shop to have the damage repaired. It should be ready in a couple of days."

Jose' reported that the Russians were still not talking and were not asking for a lawyer. They seemed to be waiting on some action from Mitch. "We're looking at some films and are trying to spot them among the crowd at the Capitol," said Jose'. "So far, we have not been successful."

"Karen and I think we may have seen them on the TV news footage," said John. "Look for Bones and Oreo climbing the balcony wall and for Tats pushing his way through a line of policemen. It looked like Mitch's jacket on the guy close behind him."

"We'll try to get you some more footage to look at," said Todd. "Homeland Security is getting quite a collection from news photographers and even from individuals with their cell phone cameras. It's hard to keep anything secret today. We're interested in anything that might show a connection to the Capitol riot."

Trooper Weaver reported that they had executed a warrant to search the properties of Richard Fleming, aka Phlegm. They found several unregistered weapons and a couple of fully automatic AK47s. "He's being held on federal weapons charges," said Weaver. "He also had a lot of survivalist gear. It's hard to tell what he was planning. We will be trying to tie the weapons found on Mitchell to him."

Trooper Cooper handed a slip of paper to Karen. "This is the name and address of the couple who relayed your lipstick message and helped get us on your trail," he said. "I thought you might like to contact them to thank them for what they did. They're a great couple."

"Thank you. I'd like to meet them personally whenever that becomes possible. I was fortunate that they took my message seriously. I worried that the finder would think it was a prank."

The Chief seemed pleased that progress was being made on several fronts. He adjourned the meeting and suggested they meet again in two days.

CHAPTER 71

Karen and John found another message waiting for them in their room. They were both to be tested for covid. When they replied to the message, they learned that someone would come to their suite at a convenient time. They set the time for 4 PM. That would give them time for their planned sightseeing walk.

"Let's skip the room service lunch and look for some food along the way," said Karen.

"Sounds good to me," said John. "I was beginning to get tired of your non-cooking anyways."

For that remark he received a gentle poke in the ribs. They made sure they had their masks and headed out for their sight-seeing.

They were careful to avoid contact with people as they exited the hotel. Karen's training gave her insight as to how far they could push the limits of their quarantine.

They found that the chamber of commerce guidebook in their hotel was accurate. There were certainly a lot of restaurants in the area. They found a small deli that was inviting and went in for their lunch. After looking extensively at the menu, they each chose the same thing. Alcoholic drinks were available, but they each chose a soft drink. They were beginning to learn some details about each other. What didn't fall into place they learned through conversation.

The day was beautiful, and the company couldn't have been better. They walked for over two hours, stopping occasionally to look at something in a store window. They mostly resisted loading up on snack food. It was nice to learn that each of them was into healthy eating. John showed one weakness though. When they looked in the window of a bakery, he couldn't help himself. He had to go in and buy some chocolate chip cookies. Karen made a mental note of this. She had a killer recipe for them. She planned to make some for him at the first opportunity. Oh, how she hoped that opportunity would come.

When they got back to the hotel they stopped into the little shop and bought a newspaper. Karen picked out a paper-back book for herself. In her nursing job, with its long hours of late, she had little time to enjoy reading. John took notice of what she chose. He was pleased to see that she read adventure novels. She chose the newest in a series by one of his favorite authors. He planned to read it when she got finished.

When they got back to their suite and stepped into the room, they automatically both looked at the phone. For once the message light was not blinking. John took Karen's hand as they walked to the sofa. They stood for the longest time in a tender embrace. When they finally sat, it was John who spoke first.

"I really enjoyed our walk. I don't believe I remember ever doing something like that before," he said. "My life was regimented to a completely different pattern in the military. Of course, I had more free time when I was stateside, but I chose to spend most all of that with my mother. I was the only light in her gradually darkening existence. She lived through an endless stream of doctors and medicines in order to spend time with me on the rare occasions I could be there. She had a few friends, but she didn't seem to enjoy that social contact so much as her illness progressed."

John hesitated as he thought about that part of his life. "At the end," he said, "all she could do was squeeze my hand."

Karen gave John a hug and squeezed his hand as they sat side by side on the sofa.

"I've seen that moment, that last moment of love and caring many times as a nurse," said Karen. "Death is one of the most difficult parts of life we see. When it happens as you describe it, we absorb some of the love that emanates from the people involved. While it can be hard on us, it can also be uplifting to know that we helped ease the process for the one dying. You did that for your mother. I'm sure there were nurses that helped both you and her in those last moments."

"You are a caring person, Karen," he said. "There were several of her nurses on that shift who helped see us through. I never thought of it the way you just expressed. I wish mother had been able to get to know you. I'm sure she would have liked you."

"I wish I could have been there for both of you, John," she said.

"I'm sorry I dragged you into this deep conversation," he said. "I guess my feelings were stimulated today by us being together in a non-stressful situation."

"I'm happy that you shared that part of yourself with me," she said. "It gave me a glimpse into your soul, and I liked the man I saw."

They cuddled on the sofa for a long time after that until they were interrupted by a knock at the door. It was the visiting nurse arriving to do the covid testing. She was a pleasant matronly lady who explained what she was about to do and did it quickly. She was gone in only a few minutes after explaining that theirs was a priority test. They would have the results sometime tomorrow.

"You seemed to be quite taken by her John," said Karen. "Are you attracted to all nurses?" she asked.

"Yes, I must admit I was stimulated by the way she stuck that stick up my nose," said John. "It makes me wonder what *you* might be capable of."

I can do that and more," said Karen. "It all comes with the package. Are you still interested?"

"Very much so," answered John. "I like the way you are packaged very much."

"If we're talking about packages, the feeling is mutual," said Karen. "I can see how yours could fit very well into my future."

"Me too," said John.

They spent some more quality time together on the sofa, talking and generally getting to know each other. After a while John said he wanted to try out the hotel's exercise facility. He went into his room and changed into his work-out clothes. When he emerged, Karen had started reading her book.

"I'll see you shortly," he said as he headed out.

"Enjoy your workout," she said. "We can order dinner when you get back."

John returned about an hour later.

"I'll grab a quick shower while you order dinner. Pick something good. I worked up an appetite," he said.

John was just soaping up when the shower door opened, and Karen stepped in.

"I decided dinner could wait," she said. "I nearly forgot my nursing duty of giving your back a scrub."

John looked at her and asked, "Do you dress like that when you help all of your patients with their showers?"

"No, only with the special ones," she answered.

* * * * *

As they were enjoying their dinner, Karen asked John how his conversation with his friend in Jamestown went.

"It was interesting," said John. "I told him in some detail what had happened, starting with the time we met and continuing on to the present."

"Only you John," he had said. "We've been through some scrapes together, but certainly nothing like that."

"I told him I wanted to opt out of his offer and that I needed to see this through with you. He understood and wished me the best. He said I should call him if I changed my mind. He's a good friend. I thanked him for being that."

"I have mixed feelings, John," she said. "I feel bad that I caused you to have to change your plans for the future, but, on the other hand, I'm happy that you did. I can't imagine how things might have turned out without you."

It was another emotional moment for Karen. John took hold of her hand until she composed herself.

"My car should be ready soon," she said. "When we can leave, I hope you will be coming back to the farm with me. Mom extended the invitation. She is looking forward to meeting you under better conditions. The same holds true with Kurt. We would be within reasonable driving distance to come back here if needed for further legal preliminaries, or for a trial when necessary."

"I hoped you would ask," said John. "I don't know how I'll pay my way, but I'll come up with something. I've often thought I might be suited for a career in law enforcement. I'll be looking into that. I have a lot of contacts through my former associates. Something should work out."

"Mom will be pleased," said Karen. "I'll call her tomorrow so she can plan for us. I'm also going to call the hospital in Gainesville. I have a lot to tell them. I'll ask for a leave of absence until this is all settled, and my future is determined."

After dinner they talked about the upcoming trip to Pennsylvania. Neither of them wanted to rush over the roads. If they had time, they wanted to see more of some parts of Ohio they passed through on the way to Toledo.

John was concerned about what kind of work he could do to help on the farm. It would all be new to him.

"Well, for starters you can shovel out the manure from the milking stalls and the calf pens in the lower part of the barn," said Karen. "That's where most of us have started. I'm sure you'll excel at that."

"The way you tell it I can almost smell it," said John. "What can I look forward to when I finish that?"

"That depends on what Kurt needs done. He always has winter work to do in preparing the fields for this year's crops. He will make sure the field drains are all in working order. Some fields must be disced, while others need plowed first. After that, the manure you shoveled will be spread on the fields. Fences need repaired or replaced. Posts need to be replaced where they are rotted. Equipment must be maintained. At a minimum that involves oil and grease, lots of grease."

"It must keep Kurt busy balancing all that," said John.

"Oh, that's not all of it. Don't forget Daisy. She needs milked twice daily. Mom usually does that, but not always. Kurt usually butchers a beef once each winter for the family, and more often if he has a customer for one. Keeping our butcher shop clean and in compliance for the inspection usually falls to Mom. She plants a garden each year and tends to her chickens. She has egg orders every other week from some steady customers. If Kurt is working late, which he often is, Sheila and the kids will come over and have dinner at the farm. She and

Mom work that out as far as the meal preparation goes. That's one thing I will do for them while we are there."

"She can cook," thought John. "This is looking better and better."

"How much of that work did you learn to do, Karen?" he asked. "It seems that it would be hard work."

"It is hard work, but I learned to work at a young age. I mowed the lawn from the time I was able to control the lawn mower. Dad even taught me how to do the maintenance on it. I helped Mom with the housework when I wasn't needed in the fields. I am two years older than Kurt, so I did a lot of what he does now, helping Dad."

"I can see how farm children would learn a work ethic that escaped the rest of us. How were you ever able to break away, so to speak, and go to nurse's training?"

"I wanted to be a nurse, and my parents wanted that for me. Kurt stepped up and took on the role I had, and I left at age eighteen. Things were going well at the farm when I graduated and found a job in Gainesville, where I had my training. I was able to get my nursing degree, working a schedule that permitted the extra study. I was planning to keep going and become a nurse practitioner, but that's when Dad took ill. I almost quit and returned to the farm, but Kurt and Mom assured me they had things under control. They downsized the beef herd to a more manageable size and Kurt went from full time to part time as a driver. I still feel guilty about not returning, but they were insistent. If I can get a good nursing job in Pennsylvania, I will probably make the move. An extra pair of hands, even part time, would make a big difference."

John hesitated as he digested all of that. He was about to speak when Karen said, "I suppose you're wondering how I came to be in Florida when there are plenty of opportunities for nurse's training in Pennsylvania."

"That thought had crossed my mind, but I figured we would eventually get to that in our discussions about our pasts. There are a lot of things you still don't know about me. I'm sure we will get to all of it as time passes."

"I followed a man," said Karen. "We were high school sweethearts, and he was going to Florida on a football scholarship. I was a farm girl with stars in her eyes. He blew his knee out as a freshman and became bitter when he learned he couldn't play football again. I tried to help him keep it together, but he wouldn't have it. He dropped out of college and out of my life. I haven't seen him since."

"I can see that life hasn't been easy for you, Karen," he said. "We have that in common. I hope I can land on my feet as well as you have. You have what it takes."

CHAPTER 72

Mitch was nervous as a cat. He could see his value to the investigation. Other than the Boss himself and possibly his lawyer, Mitch knew more about the criminal operations of Mr. Wade Dilmore, aka the Boss than any living person. How that knowledge would balance against Mitch's culpability in those matters, as well as his own problems with the kidnapping was yet to be determined.

There was also the matter of the US Capitol. That was probably a federal crime. He planned to keep that out of his conversation, if at all possible.

Two PM came and went. Each tick of the clock past the appointed time caused the level of pain in his gut to increase. He wanted this to be over.

Finally, at twenty past two the agents appeared at his cell door.

"Sorry we're late," said Stewell. "We got tied up in a meeting. How are you holding up?"

"Not too well," answered Mitch. "I may need you to have a Doc get me something for my stomach."

"That's not an unusual condition for someone in your position. Hopefully, you'll feel better after this session," said Stewell. "In any case, we'll have someone get something for you."

"I have here the document in which you grant this interview without your attorney being present," said Connie. "Once you sign it, keeping a copy for yourself, we can begin."

Mitch read the short document and signed It without comment. "One more thing," said Stewell. "We will be recording this session. We will not however, be sending a copy to your attorney, under the circumstances. You may request a copy for a new attorney, or for yourself if you so choose."

They went through the procedures of identifying themselves on the recording.

"You called for this meeting, Mr. Mitchell. What did you have in mind?" asked Connie.

"I want a deal," said Mitch. "I am fifty-six years old, and I have been working for Wade Dilmore since I was fourteen. I have knowledge of all his business ventures, some legal, mostly not. I am a walking history book of his operations. Much of the money he handled was off the books. I can provide the information that will show the proof of all that. His operations extended into several states and should therefore come under your jurisdiction."

"That all sounds good," said Connie. "It would certainly be helpful to us. I'm sure we could work out something for you in exchange for that, but what about the kidnapping charges. It led to the shooting incident in which one of your men lost his life. The law is clear on that. You can be held responsible to some extent for that as well. I'm not certain we could justify that to our supervisors unless you have something extraordinary to offer."

Mitch started to sweat. He had been hoping that what he offered would wipe the slate clean, but the way she explained it, he now had serious doubts. "The one who died, 'Dinny' didn't have anyone. He had no living relatives that I know of, and the women he associated with will not miss him. I know that doesn't matter under the law. A life is a life. I just wanted you to know that. Bolo and I were the closest that he had to 'family'. What if I had something else to offer? Something *big,* I mean national headlines *big?*"

"Everything has value Mr. Mitchell," said Connie. "What would you hope to get in return for this new information?"

"If I give you *anything* and still go to prison, my life could be worth a pack of cigarettes, maybe less. If I give you the whole package, I want 'witness protection.' If I can't get that and I continue with my lawyer, who is also the Boss's lawyer, I get a second-rate defense. My rights and needs will be subordinate to those of the Boss. If I change lawyers, the Boss will think I'm putting my needs first. Again, I may not be worth that pack of cigarettes."

"Let's just say that you make a good case for making a deal with us. To move forward with this, we are going to need some hint of what your *big value* information is. What can you tell us?"

"I know who is behind the riot at the US Capitol," said Mitch, "and it's not Donald Trump."

"Mr. Mitchell, if you have that information and you have proof to support it, you are holding a good hand. We will need to confer with our supervisors on this and get back to you."

"You are good at document writing," said Mitch. "Bring me the document I am looking for and we can get started with the debriefing."

CHAPTER 73

"What do you think Connie?" asked Chick. "This could break the case wide open if he has what he says he has."

"I agree. This is an intelligent man. It's a shame he chose the life path he did. He could have made something of himself. Maybe he didn't have much of a choice."

"I'll schedule a conference call with headquarters and see how they feel about giving him his deal," said Chick. "I'm looking forward to seeing his proof. We should probably get Todd involved in this too."

CHAPTER 74

Jimmy Sylvan had been the Boss's lawyer for over thirty years. He had other clients, but none of them provided him the income that his relationship with Wade Dilmore had. Defending him was about to be the challenge of his legal career. He'd had to walk a fine line with the law in several cases involving Dilmore, but none like this. It would all be on the line with this one.

When Jimmy learned some of what happened at the warehouse, he knew it was serious. He would be representing the Boss, no question about that. But the boss wanted him to represent Mitch also. That could be a conflict of interest. He tried to explain to the Boss, but to no avail.

Jimmy believed that *information* was the key to his success as a defense lawyer. One person who had helped him in the past was a local private investigator named Nat McElhenny. Nat was good at his job, and he wasn't afraid to step over the edge when necessary. The Boss was good for a bonus in those instances. He called Nat and told him what he needed.

When Jimmy met with Mitch in his cell, his instincts set off alarms more than ever. Mitch was caught in the middle in this case, and as such was a huge threat. He would be expected to roll over and play dead as needed in the Boss's defense effort. Jimmy didn't trust that he would do that.

Nat had given him a bug that was designed to look like a bolt head. When he got the opportunity, he placed the bug high up on the top steel frame member of the cell. He didn't monitor it at that stage, but when he got the flimsy excuse from Mitch that he wanted to postpone the meeting with him, he called Nat.

* * * * * *

Nat sat in his van a block away from the east wall of the lockup facility. He had done this type of surveillance many times. Usually, it was the most boring job one could imagine. Today was different. The bells were ringing in his head like the jackpot bells in a casino. This was a big one. He loaded the recording onto a thumb drive. Usually, he erased the recording at this point. Instead, this time he made a second thumb drive. This one would go into his safe. That one would be his life insurance.

"Jimmy, this is Nat. You were right. He's going to sing. I have it all, clear as a bell. I'll drop it off to you on my way back to the office."

Nat could almost imagine what size of bonus would come his way. It would be way more than enough to keep his beard groomed for the rest of his life.

CHAPTER 75

The next 10 AM meeting proved to be interesting. The Chief had been coordinating the investigation of the evidence found in the warehouse. Trooper Cooper had brought in a forensic accountant from the Ohio State Police. He was able to make sense of some of what was found in the office safe, but much of it was foreign to him.

"What we have," said the Chief, are records of several illicit businesses. Most of them are operating in Michigan, in Detroit in particular. Dilmore was apparently involved in gambling, prostitution, drug trafficking, and even counterfeiting.

"Do we need to bring in Treasury on this?" asked Stewell. "That last one falls within their jurisdiction."

"We're not sure yet," said the Chief. "Most of what we found were fake liquor tax stamps. A print shop in Michigan was making those. We found that Dilmore owned several night clubs. From what we have been able to piece together, he imported moonshine liquor from at least three producers in Pennsylvania and West Virginia. We surmise that he had the legitimate stuff on display but poured the illegal for his customers."

"I can take that a step further," said Trooper Cooper. "Our forensic accountant got here yesterday. He was able to spot a familiar face among the photos in the blackmail files. It was the owner of a Pennsylvania trucking company. It looks like we'll be able to tie in the trucking pickup and delivery routes to the transporting of the alcohol."

"We have an investigator from the Detroit police force arriving later today. They are also sending their forensic accountant," said the Chief. "With all these pencil pushers we should be able to make some sense out of all of this. The trucking company throws an interesting light on the case. It provides a plausible scenario for the ability of Dilmore's operations to reach into other states."

"I just had a thought," said John. "Jose', when you and Trooper Weaver compare notes on our friend Richard Fleming, it might be interesting to see if there were any pickup or delivery stops at his location by our trucking company."

"Good idea, John," said Jose'.

"Ditto from me," said Weaver. "We suspect that Phlegm is a middle-man in some small-scale gun running. This could be the link we're looking for."

"What about our friend Mitch?" asked Connie. "Are you able to tie him into any of these illegal operations?"

"We're confident that we will be," said the chief. "There are many references to "M" in the paperwork. We suspect that is Mitchell. The accountants should be able to tie those in with upcoming witness testimonies. We think Mitchell was the bag man for Dilmore. They usually will be able to prove his movements in relationship to the deposits of money on Dilmore's end and the testimonies on the pickup end."

"That squares with what our accountant tells us," said Stewell. "We have good interagency cooperation on this, but the nature of the case will probably mean some overlapping work. It's hard to imagine how Dilmore kept track of it all."

"Chick and Connie are working on a possible deal with Mitchell," said Todd. "I can't go into detail yet, as it involves my agency also. I'll have to get the okay from the higher-ups before it can go into effect. If it does, it will make everyone's job a lot easier. Mitchell is in this up to his neck. He's a valuable link in almost everything we're talking about."

The conversations dealt with a variety of minor details after that. The Chief adjourned the meeting and asked John to remain for a few minutes before he left. Karen said she would see John back at the suite.

"John, you have proven again that you are a valuable part of this investigation. I personally want to thank you. You wouldn't have to do this, and I know it's appreciated by everyone."

"I guess it's just how my brain works," said John. "I've been able to see the bigger picture at times when it was difficult to follow the usual path. I can't explain why, it just happens."

"I may have a bit of good news for you," said the Chief. "There is at least one situation that I know of where there is some reward money available. I'm going to apply for that in your name as being the key to solving that case. I won't go into detail though, until I know if the people making the decisions see it my way. It's just possible there may be more rewards out there, as complicated as this case is. I'll let you know when I know more."

John was taken aback by this revelation. He had no idea there could be anything like this coming. He thanked the Chief and headed back to the suite. "Should I tell Karen?" thought John. "Maybe I should wait to see if it happens."

CHAPTER 76

"That didn't take long," said Karen. "I thought maybe they were going to present you with the key to the city."

"Just a pat on the back," said John. "The chief gave me his personal thanks for the help I have been able to give in the case. He's a special person. I've only run into one other like him. His attitude toward his work inspires confidence in those around him. We're fortunate to have several selfless people on the task force. With multiple agencies involved it could be a game of one-upmanship. That's not the case here."

"I have had that feeling too," said Karen. "They all seem to respect one another. They are making progress in the case, that's for sure. I'm anxious to see how the potential 'deal' turns out with Mitch. I'm curious to find out what happened before they got to the farm. If they were involved in the riot at the Capitol, that would be worth making some concessions in exchange for the truth of that. We're sure not getting the true story in the news media."

"Ditto that," said John. "I have some speculations that are probably more accurate than what they are feeding us."

Their conversation was interrupted by the ringing of their room phone. John took the call. It was from the Chief.

"I just found out, John," he said. "Karen's car will be finished early tomorrow. The repairs have been made. The paint will be drying over- night. They tell me it looks as good as new. I'll have it delivered to you around 9 AM. I'm also going to send over Karen's weapon and her mother's rifle. Neither of them is important to the case. The other personal items that were in the car will still be there. Please sign the accompanying receipts for our records. Maybe you can get out for a ride and see a little of our city."

"That's a good idea, Chief. I think we'll do that. Thanks for everything."

John told Karen the good news that the Chief had relayed. They spent the next couple of hours planning their day for tomorrow.

*   *   *   *   *

John and Karen were up early in anticipation for their day of sightseeing. The car arrived on schedule. All the things that were in the car when it was impounded were there. They signed the papers and were ready to go.

"I can't believe how good the car looks," said Karen. "I guess the Florida sun had gradually dulled the paint. It's like new again."

"I was hoping they would leave a couple of the bullet holes in it," said John. "They would have enhanced our image in Bullskin Township when we tell our story."

"I hadn't thought of that. I'm sure the local reporters will be on our doorstep when we get back. We should probably discuss what our story will be with Todd and the FBI. I wouldn't want to jeopardize their deal with Mitch."

"That's a good idea," said John. "It looks like Mitch's knowledge could blow the lid off the entire investigation. I hope they give him some extra protection when his employer finds out Mitch is turning on him."

"I almost feel sorry for him, almost, but not quite. It will be a while until I forget what he put me through. I know I'll relive some of it when I see my mother again. I need to know she is okay before I can begin to forgive Mitch."

"I only was with her for a matter of minutes," said John, "but my impression is that your mother is a strong woman. She didn't wilt when she saw them take you. She knew what she had to do to help when I said I would go after you. Kurt did too. They worked together and got me on the road as quickly as possible."

Karen was in thought for a while as she processed what John had said.

"You seem to know how to bring me out of a blue funk, John. I think I could go for a man like you. Let's go see Toledo."

Before they could get out the door the phone rang. It was the nurse with the results of their covid tests. They were both 'negative.'

"Now we can enjoy this day as a celebration of sorts," said John. "I wasn't concerned that either of us might test positive, but one never knows."

CHAPTER 77

They drove through the city at a leisurely pace, stopping at points of interest. The weather was cooperating. They enjoyed views of the Maumee River, which later became the Maumee Bay and Lake Erie. With no route or destination in mind, they found themselves heading north in the direction of Detroit. They exited I-75 at any given opportunity, or at any time a view of the lake presented itself. After taking a loop around Detroit, they headed west toward Ann Arbor. There they saw a city built around a university (U. of Michigan). There were beautiful upscale neighborhoods and inviting business districts. It was easy to see why many executives and professionals chose to live in Ann Arbor and commute to their work in surrounding cities. They had dinner there before heading back to Toledo.

"Let's take another loop around Toledo," said Karen. "I want to see the city at night. The view from our hotel at night is nothing short of spectacular, but I would like to complete the picture and see the lights along the river."

"Me too," said John. "This could be the last chance to do this if things keep moving as quickly as they are now."

When they got back to their suite, Karen asked John what he meant by this being their last chance to see the lights of the city.

"I've been wondering if it is necessary for us to be quarantined for the entire ten days if we intend to leave immediately afterwards. We can establish a computer link and still be present at the task force meetings. There is no need now for our physical presence. I feel that we are treading water as far as advancing our plans for each other. I don't think the task force members will object. They can have their meeting at the Chief's headquarters and cut costs. They were probably having it here to accommodate us. What do you think?"

"You seem to have read my mind again, John."

"No big deal," he said. "Blondes are easy."

Before John could make another such comment, Karen had bounced a pillow off his head.

"It will probably be quite a while before we have to return for a trial," said John. "If it is tried in a federal court, it may not even be held in Toledo. From here on, I want it to be all about us. We'll work them in when we have to."

"There you go again, with the mind-reading." Karen responded this time with a patented 'Grant woman' hug.

They talked about their contrived plans for the rest of the evening. A decision was made to rise early and talk to the Chief. If he gave his blessings to their plan, they could check out tomorrow and be on their way.

"I would like to follow the route through the Ohio countryside that Mitch took if that's okay with you," said Karen. "I have negative feelings about all of that and retracing that route may help me overcome some of it. I will definitely be travelling with better company."

"Me too," said John. "I was in a hurry when I went through some of those places. I would like to enjoy seeing them with you beside me rather than somewhere in front of me. I prefer the entire picture, to the more distant view of the back of your head."

"You certainly do have a way with words, Captain Osmond. Now I have an idea of how we can spend our last night in this gorgeous hotel."

* * * * *

John was on the phone with the Chief early enough to catch him before he got involved in his day's duties. He presented his ideas to him about the early departure. The Chief listened to him without comment as John covered all the bases.

"It sounds to me like you've worked out all the details of your plan," said the Chief. "I don't see any reason for you to stay here any longer. I'll alert the rest of the task force, and with your permission I'll give them your phone numbers if any question should arise. Otherwise, your idea of a communications link into our meetings is good. I'm sure the others will agree to that. Your testimonies in a trial will probably be necessary, but we don't know how far off that will be. There will undoubtedly be depositions once the lawyers get involved, but that can probably be done in Pennsylvania as a convenience to you."

"I don't remember when I've had as much satisfaction working with anyone as I have had with you and Karen. Others on the task force have made similar comments. Working with you on the details of the crimes has made our jobs much easier, believe me, much easier. Get in touch with my office when you are ready to set up the link. In the meantime, enjoy your drive back to Pennsylvania."

John and Karen each said their goodbyes to the Chief and expressed their thanks for the accommodations provided by the city.

John phoned the hotel manager and told him of their plans to leave. He asked them to sign out as guests of the city before leaving. John wanted to leave gratuities for the staff, and for Amy in particular. The manager refused that, saying that it had all been covered.

* * * * *

As they left Toledo, they passed the warehouse complex where Mitch attempted to divert John's pursuit. It deserved only a passing comment this time. They did not attempt to take the circuitous route that had been originally followed.

As they travelled south on US Route 23 their memories of various landmarks evoked comments of their separate experiences during the original trip. At Fostoria they turned onto state Route 18 toward Tiffin. That leg of the trip was where John became aware that his pursuit had been discovered.

They followed Route 18 toward Bellevue. When they got to the Flat Rock area, Karen remembered some of the details of where the white van was abandoned. As they relived their experiences of that event, John recalled how he observed the switching of the vehicles. He described how he watched the theft from a different location in the dealership lot. Karen's memory allowed her to confirm what he saw as well as add some detail that he couldn't see.

John started to comment, then suddenly he stopped in mid-sentence. He pulled off the road and looked at Karen.

"I think I might know what Mitch meant when he said the words, 'arm rest' before he blacked out," said John. "We thought he may have been referring to a possible hiding place of something in the Pacifica. What if he was talking about an arm rest in the white van? We didn't think of that."

"That's a possibility," said Karen. "When he secured my hands, he always fastened me to the back of the front seat. There was a secure grip there as an aid to the back seat passenger. He could have chosen to attach me to the arm rest on the door. It would have worked just as well. Maybe he was afraid I would pull it loose."

"The van is probably still in an impound lot somewhere nearby. I'm going to call Todd to see if he knows."

John phoned Todd. He caught him preparing to return to Chicago. When he explained his revelation to Todd, he agreed that it should be checked out. "The Ohio State Police have the van," said Todd. "I'll call them and find out where it is. I'll get back to you."

"They have it at a state police barracks lot near where you are now," said Todd. "They haven't done anything with it so far. Would you have time to check it out for us? We wouldn't expect you to do any major tear-down work on it. Just have a look at the area you suspect."

John agreed to go to the barracks and check the arm rests of the van. It might be a waste of time, but maybe not. Todd had arranged for him to meet Sergeant McLaughlin at the barracks.

Karen spotted the van in a fenced-in area behind the barracks as they pulled into the parking lot. She had a little twinge of fear as she saw it, but that quickly disappeared.

Sergeant McLaughlin was watching for them and met them at the door as they approached the building. He had a collection of screw drivers in his hand.

"Agent Farley told me you might want to remove an arm rest in the van. Maybe one of these will do the job."

When they entered the compound John said, "Let's try the back door on the driver's side. That's the one Karen thinks might be the one."

John got to his knees and looked up at the underside of the armrest. "Is one of those screwdrivers a 'torx' style?" he asked.

"Try this," said the Sergeant.

"That's the one," said John as he inserted the tool into the recessed hole under the armrest.

In less than a minute the screws were removed, and John tugged on the armrest to break the seal that help hold it in place. When he did, he felt something drop into the palm of his hand.

"I think we found what we are looking for," said John as he held out his hand for the others to see.

He was holding a small computer thumb drive.

"Bring that into my office," said the Sergeant. "It must be something important for him to hide it like that."

They went into the barracks where the Sergeant took them to the dispatcher's desk. There was an attractive blond lady seated in front of the terminal.

"This is our dispatcher, Pattycakes. Let's see if she can download what you found into our computer. If it's encrypted, we may have a problem."

Pattycakes inserted the drive into her computer, and it opened. "It's some sort of meeting," she said. "I'm downloading it now. I don't know how long the file is, so it may take a few minutes."

The Sergeant invited Karen and John into his office while they waited. John told a little of how the case was progressing and explained what led them to the targeted search in the van. After a few minutes, Pattycakes came into the office. She had a serious look on her face.

"I think you should listen to this," she said.

She handed the drive to the Sergeant. He inserted it into his computer. Pattycakes had one of the other officers take her station so she could remain in the office.

"What's wrong?" asked the Sergeant. "You look like you've seen a ghost."

"Just listen to some of this and you'll see."

As the four of them listened, they became quiet. Jaws dropped and heads shook as they realized they were listening to a plan for the Capitol riot. Karen was able to recognize Mitch's voice.

After hearing about a half hour of the recorded 'minutes' of the meeting, Sergeant McLaughlin stopped the replay. "We're getting near the end of the workday, and I want to get a copy of this forwarded to Todd Farley as soon as possible," he said. "If everything here is for real, Mitchell's life is probably in danger. They will want to have extra security protecting him right away. Pattycakes, forward this to Farley, then make two copies of it. One copy will be for us to take home with us tonight and the other will be for John to take with him. In the meantime, I suggest that what we have heard here stays with the four of us. This is a hot potato. We need to keep it contained."

"You can trust Karen and me," said John. "Our top priority is the successful resolution of this case."

"You can trust Pattycakes and me as well. I take her home with me. I should have told you she is my wife."

CHAPTER 78

Mitch was nearing the completion of another long, boring day. He could not imagine having to spend the rest of his life in confinement. One of his small pleasures was his scheduled time in the shower. His was an early evening time slot. This allowed him to relax after his meal before bedtime. The shower seemed to help wash some of his troubled thoughts away, at least for a while.

As he stood under the hot water, he was startled to hear a voice behind his ear.

"Where is it?" the voice asked. "Where is the drive?"

"I don't know what you're talking about. What drive?"

"Don't give me that. The drive. The minutes. Turn off the water."

Mitch complied. When the water was off, he turned around. What he saw was one of the largest men he had ever encountered. He was probably about 6'6" tall and went at least four hundred pounds. He was holding a homemade knife. It had a crude looking blade, but Mitch was certain it could do the job for which it was intended.

Mitch had known real fear only a few times in his life, and those were in his teen years. The man was fully clothed, and he had a deadly look on his face. Mitch instantly shriveled. He was a dead man. He was sure of it.

"I..I don't have it with me," stammered Mitch.

"Well now, that I can *see*," said the huge man. "Tell me where it is, and you can go on living."

Mitch made a quick decision to let his fear win. He would take his chances after that. "I hid it in the van I was driving," said Mitch. It's inside the armrest of the seat behind the driver's seat. I had to ditch the van coming to Toledo. The cops probably have it now. I stole the car they caught me in back in Bellevue. It's probably still where I hid it. I can't see them going that far in searching the car. We emptied it of everything else when we switched. I just forgot the drive."

"You know, I believe you. That sounds wild enough to be true. Where can I find the van and what does it look like?"

Mitch described the white van in as much detail as he could. He told the man where they had ditched it and suggested that it was probably impounded at the nearest state police barracks.

"I've given you what you want," said Mitch. "Now, I want to live. I can keep my mouth shut."

"That's not what I heard," said the man. He spun Mitch around and raised an arm, intending to plunge the knife into him through his armpit and into his heart. Mitch saw this coming and instantly lowered himself a few inches. With the height difference of the two combatants, the angle of the thrust was diverted just enough to miss the heart. The damage was severe however, and Mitch slumped instantly to the floor of the shower in a heap, his blood forming a trail toward the drain. The assassin wiped his prints from the weapon and dropped it to the floor. If they discovered him in a place where he shouldn't be, he didn't want it on his person. He left quickly, before the guard was due.

CHAPTER 79

John and Karen followed the route back to the Ohio Turnpike. They were each quiet in their thoughts of what they had heard about the planning of the Capitol Riot. This revelation answered the question of why Mitch had chosen to stop at a private home with Dinny rather than a hospital or urgent care facility. His motley crew would stand out at a public facility. Questions would be asked. He couldn't afford that. He also had illegal weapons in the van. Karen and John discussed this as they headed east.

"They told Mom that Dinny had been sick just before they stopped at the farm," said Karen. "I guess it was just bad luck that they chose the Grant farm. There are a number of other places they could have stopped along the route they were on."

"It may have been Grant bad luck, but it proved to be a bad choice for Mitch too," said John. "Your family certainly made things difficult for him. It's likely that any other place he may have chosen would have been more of a pushover. He's probably been kicking himself ever since he met the Grants."

"You're too kind, John. Don't you think you had something to do with his downfall yourself?"

"Well, maybe a little. But only because I met the formidable Grant daughter."

As they travelled eastward, Karen had thoughts of how her family would be after the ordeal they had been through. She knew the arrival of John and her would certainly go a long way toward healing any scars that might remain. Kurt should be near the end of his quarantine period. Hopefully, they could have a big family dinner to celebrate the several positive changes in their lives. It would be a good way for John to meet the rest of the family.

Karen had always been one to have a plan for her path forward in life. She had suffered the break-up of her early romance a few years back, but other than that, she had a view of where she was headed. Since John had come into her life, she seemed to have lost that vision into her future. She could see several obstacles in the path. So far John had proven capable of overcoming those obstacles. They had quickly grown closer and more determined to help build a life together. She could not even imagine going back to the life she had before John.

While Karen was absorbed in her thoughts, John let his mind wander to his future. His early life had not prepared him for interaction with others in a close familial relationship. His mother was the only person he had. There was a lot missing in the way of experiences that he now wished he had. How would he be accepted by Karen's family? He was about as well prepared for what was ahead of him as a teenager on a first date. His military training didn't help him much here.

"John," said Karen. "Let's talk about our future. The last few days have been an emotional roller-coaster ride for me. I'm not used to life moving at such a pace. I know we care a lot about each other, and I am having difficulty getting a clear picture of where we are heading. How do you see things developing for us?"

"I'm right beside you in that roller-coaster. It seems that we are reading each other's minds again. We're about to face the first important thing in our common future. That's meeting your family. I'm not afraid of much, but I must admit that I'm worried about that. What if they don't like me?"

Karen smiled at that and said, "Scratch that one off your list John, they're going to love you. I'm sure of that."

"We have the matter of our different career paths," said John. "You are well on your way to a professional career in nursing, while I'm at a crossroads. I have been thinking of looking at a career in law enforcement. That could make use of some of my military background, or I could start over, in something completely different. I know one thing for certain, I want to be near you. From that first minute when we decided I would come with you to the farm, I wanted to be there for you. That has been the case throughout this entire ordeal. It has been the most meaningful thing I have done in my life. I want to continue being there for you."

"I want that too, John. I want that very much."

They rode on in silence for a while, each absorbed in dreams of their future. They were nearing the end of the Ohio Turnpike when Karen suggested they take a different route back to the farm.

"I'd like to go back on Route 422 John. If you don't mind, I want us to have one more night together, just the two of us. We can stop at a motel in the Youngstown area for the night. We could listen to the rest of the material on the flash drive this evening while there are not others around. This route will take us past some picturesque parts of Pennsylvania, and we will get back at a more convenient time for Mom."

"Those are good ideas, Karen," said John. "Why don't you expand the GPS screen to see if you can find the connecting route to 422. I'm also anxious to hear the rest of what's on the flash drive. We should be able to download it into my laptop."

Karen plotted the route through Youngstown, and they found a motel along Route 422 just before the Pennsylvania border. After checking in they had dinner at a nearby restaurant.

"I can't imagine what might be on that recording," said Karen. "I have been so involved in my nursing work with its increased demands that I haven't had much time to follow politics. It doesn't seem possible that something like this could happen in our country. We hear about them occurring in other parts of the world, but I always assumed our system of government was above that sort of thing."

"I know what you mean," said John. "When I was deployed, I saw the results of political upheaval. My life was centered around it. Now, I almost feel betrayed that this happened here. You develop a sense of security when you serve in the military. It helps you be able to do your job in a foreign country if you have pride in the way things are run back home. I've had concerns about what we hear on the news lately, but I had no idea we had gone this far astray. I'm afraid we may not like what we hear on the rest of that recording."

Their dinner conversation had put a damper on their evening plans. When they returned to the motel, the first thing they did was listen to the recording on the flash drive. Karen again identified Mitch's voice in the early part, and with his questions near the end. Since John had only heard him briefly, from a distance in the barn he wouldn't have been able to so quickly identify him.

When they had heard it all, they sat quietly for a while. John could tell that Karen was deeply affected by what they heard. She had come to an understanding of the kidnapping based on the assumption of how the events unfolded at the farm. Dinny had the virus. Mitch made the choice to involve the Grant family. Mitch's plans were disrupted, and he chose to take her along when the remainder of his gang fled the scene.

Now, with this new revelation of what had occurred prior to the gang coming to the farm, Karen's thoughts were confused. She could see that Mitch had a lot more motivation to do what he had done. It wasn't just about Dinny. He had a lot more at risk than only the virus. He had played a part in a major conspiracy, the riot at the US Capitol.

John was at a loss for words. He didn't know what to say to help Karen deal with her mixed-up emotions. He was sure she was feeling some of the same things as he was, that any patriotic American would. A mixture of anger and frustration would best describe it. In a sense the attack on the Capitol felt like an attack on him personally. The frustration part came from not being able to do anything about it.

As John sat beside Karen on the bed, he had one arm around her to help comfort her as she dealt with her own mixed emotions. In his other hand he held the thumb drive that exposed a major attack on his country.

"I've got to do something about this," thought John. "This has to be exposed. I've got to find a way to do it."

CHAPTER 80

The guard headed toward the prison showers. Mitch's time was up. He would escort him back to his cell in solitary and get the next prisoner on the schedule.

When he got to the small dressing area, Mitchell was not there. He stuck his head around the corner and said, "Get a move on Mitchell. Your time's up."

When there was no response, he stepped into the shower and saw Mitch splayed on the floor with a blood trail to the drain. He was on his radio immediately as he hurried to check Mitch for a pulse.

"He's still breathing. I've got a pulse," the guard reported. "It looks like someone put a shiv into him. He needs an ambulance stat."

While he waited for the ambulance another guard came to assist. They were able to stop the flow of blood and secure the weapon.

"This looks like a professional hit," said the second guard. "I've seen one like this before. A knife just below the armpit usually hits the heart. Mitchell was lucky. This guy just missed his target."

The ambulance crew arrived and prepared Mitch for transport. The hospital was not too far away. Next on the scene was the warden. The shower was getting crowded. The warden was quiet until the ambulance left, then he spoke to the two guards.

"I just got a call about Mitchell," he said. "Suddenly he is a high-profile witness. They want him to have twenty-four-hour security and no visitors. The call came a little too late for him. You two are to talk with nobody about this. This is an information lock-down. If the assassin learns that he botched the job, he may try again. Cancel the shower schedule for the rest of the evening until the evidence techs can get through in here."

The warden didn't look forward to the conversation he would have with the Chief. Sometimes you just couldn't move fast enough.

CHAPTER 81

The quick action by the guards helped to save Mitch. He was given a transfusion right away when he got to the ER. The way the doctor explained it, a quarter inch one way and his heart muscle would have been cut. A quarter inch the other way and his aorta would have been cut. There was some minor damage to a lung, but they had repaired that when they had him in surgery. Mitch was a lucky man that day. The would-be assassin, however, was not so lucky. His knife thrust barely missed being fatal.

The Chief chose two of his most trusted officers to provide security for Mitch at the hospital. He didn't want to take any chances of having another attempt being successful.

The warden ordered a search of Mitch's cell to look for a clue to how this might have happened. When the assigned officers approached the cell, they observed a convict outside the door to the cell. When the convict spotted them, he ran away. They were unable to catch him, but they believe they know who it was. It was a large man. One prisoner who fit that description was a trustee with a known drug problem. He was supposed to be off the stuff, but if someone waved cash under his nose, the temptation might have been too much.

It took them a while to find the bug. They would have looked a lot longer with just a visual search. When one of them employed an electronic detection wand, it didn't take long. The thing looked exactly like a bolt head. The warden checked the visitors log and found that Mitch had three visitors during his incarceration. The two FBI agents and *Attorney Sylvan*, who would have guessed?

The Chief made two calls to task force members. He thought it vital that Todd Farley and the FBI team be informed of the attempt on Mitch's life. If they wanted to bring in other task force members, it would be their choice. It was probably not necessary to involve anyone else at this stage.

The Chief also shared his suspicions with the federal agents. He gave details about the prison trustee, Attorney Sylvan, and about a local private investigator named Nat McElhenny. Locals used his services when they wanted a sleazy job done or when it was necessary to bend the law. He had worked for Attorney Sylvan in the past.

Todd Farley told the Chief that he had been assigned permanently to the case until it was resolved. Agent Quint would be working with him. They would establish a home base in Toledo.

"We need a couple days to clear our desks, then we will return to Toledo," said Farley. "The plan is to coordinate interagency matters through us. Agents Stewell and Palmori will be working out of our office as well."

"It will be good to have you back," said the Chief. "With Osmond finding the flash drive, things are starting to break quickly. We'll need your sources to help ID the people in the recording. I'm hoping that we'll be able to tie them in using facial recognition from the photo images of the riot. When Mitchell is recovered enough, we want to expedite his deal, if possible. He should be a valuable source of descriptions and voices. Our plan here is to be able to exert enough pressure on Dilmore to have him turn against the Washington group. I know all of that is a lot to hope for, but we've got to start somewhere."

CHAPTER 82

Karen was feeling somewhat better after breakfast. She hadn't slept well last night. Each time she awoke though, she was able to find comfort in having John beside her.

As they travelled along Route 422, John tried to help bring her back to being herself by asking questions about the areas they travelled through. The route took them through the Lake Arthur area, one of the largest lakes in western Pennsylvania. At Kittanning they crossed over the Allegheny River, which along with the Monongahela formed the Ohio River at Pittsburgh.

Karen related that many of the towns in western Pennsylvania were named for Indian tribes.

"There's a story about a tribe of Indians that lived along the river at the location of the modern-day town of Tarentum," she said. "As the story goes, there was an Indian tribe living along the river. Each Indian had one teepee. All except one, who had three teepees. One of his friends asked him why he had the two extra teepees when everyone else had only one. He answered, "Ta-rent-um." The name just sort of stuck."

John laughed. "You must be feeling better if you can tell a corny joke like that," he said.

"I am feeling better, John," she said. "Just being with you brings out the best in me."

They passed through the town of Indiana (PA), the location of Indiana University of Pennsylvania.

"Several of my high school friends came here to further their education," said Karen.

Just past Indiana, before the next town of Homer City, they changed to Route 119. Karen pointed out a 1200 ft high smokestack on the right.

"That's a coal-fired generating station," she said. "There are three in this county. It's a shame, but environmentalist politics may force them to close. Coal is the lifeblood of the economy here. It would devastate the area."

John looked around him. "It looks clean here," he said.

"It is clean, and healthy," said Karen. "The people who live here are happy. Since scrubbers were installed, most of the pollutants are removed. It all seems to be politically motivated."

"I believe it is," said John. "It looks like the next target is natural gas and oil. They don't seem to be able to see beyond their environmentally sensitive noses. Technology is not advanced enough to replace what we now have. The cart never could be efficiently *pushed* by the horse, but that's what they're trying to do."

"If you're ready for some lunch, I know a place I would like to stop. When I was home for a vacation, I would sometimes visit my college friends in Indiana. I stopped at Dean's Diner in Blairsville whenever I could. It is one of several restaurants in Pennsylvania that has a unique style of architecture. You'll like their pie."

They stopped at the diner, and the experience surpassed their expectations. Several white-clad waitresses buzzed around like a swarm of bees, chatting with customers while kibitzing with each other. Karen thought she remembered their waitress, Loretta from one of her previous trips.

"Would you like some pie," asked Loretta.

"What kind do you have," asked John.

"We have Banana, Chocolate, Coconut, Graham cracker, Lemon, Cherry Crumb, Apple, Blueberry, Cherry, Peach, Raisin, Apple Crumb, Blueberry Cream, Cherry Cream, Peanut butter Cream, Peanut butter and Chocolate Cream, Pumpkin, Peanut butter and Chocolate Banana."

"Can you say that backwards?" asked John.

"Yes," answered Loretta, as she turned her back to John and said the list again. Apparently, she had been asked that question before.

Just then, Heather came flying into the dining room like she was on roller skates and said, "I just sold the last of the Raisin."

Karen had graham cracker and John had apple.

When they left the diner, Karen said that they should be at the farm in an hour.

As they got closer to their destination, Karen's thoughts returned to the time Mitch went off course to stop for the buy at Phlegm's place. She told John what she was thinking, and he suggested they drive past the place for curiosity's sake.

"I haven't heard whether he is in custody or out on bail," he said. "If we see anything interesting, I'll report it to the task force."

As they drove past, Karen remarked," It looks just as shabby as I remember it. His truck is there, but that doesn't necessarily mean he is. They could have hauled him off to jail and left it."

"If he made a lot of money trafficking in guns, he certainly didn't spend it beautifying his property," said John.

"It would be interesting to know his history," said Karen. "He is supposed to be Bolo's cousin. Maybe crime just runs in the family."

They continued toward the farm. John remarked when they passed the point where he diverted his route and headed west on Interstate 70.

"I wonder if things would have turned out differently if I had chosen the other route through Ohio," he thought. "There's no way to know," he decided. "It doesn't pay to dwell on the past."

Karen had phoned her mother when they left Blairsville and told her their approximate time of arrival. She was only a couple of minutes off on her guess. They turned into the driveway at the farm.

CHAPTER 83

It had been a lonely week for Bolo as he recovered from his wounds at the hospital. As soon as he was well enough to get out of bed and walk for short distances, he discovered a guard outside his room. The only visitors he had were two FBI agents. He couldn't get much information from them. He only learned that Mitch had been injured and that Dinny was dead. Bolo didn't ask for legal representation when his rights were read to him. He was confident that Mitch would provide that for him as soon as he was able.

Bolo was becoming a little concerned. He was nearly recovered enough to be discharged from the hospital and he still had not heard from Mitch or from the Boss's lawyer.

Just when he was about to ask the guard outside his door to find out what was going on, he was surprised by a visit from the Boss's lawyer, Attorney Sylvan.

"Mr. Ball," said Sylvan. "I'm attorney Jimmy Sylvan. I have been retained by Wade Dilmore to represent you. How are you feeling?"

"I'm feeling about ready to get out of here, Mr. Sylvan," said Bolo. "My friends call me Bolo."

"Fine Bolo, you can call me Jimmy," Sylvan responded.

These formalities were interesting, in that these men had been aware of each other for years. It was, however, due to their vastly different levels of participation within the organization that they were effectively strangers.

"I had expected to hear from Mitch as soon as he was well enough. I don't even know how he was injured," said Bolo. "Did he arrange with the Boss for you to be here?"

"Unfortunately, no. I don't know any details yet, but I just learned that Mitch has died while he was incarcerated. I have been sent here by Mr. Dilmore to represent you. He needs your help."

Bolo was stunned. Mitch was dead. It didn't seem possible. They had been friends since they were children. Bolo had provided physical protection for Mitch while he received guidance and advice from Mitch. They had relied on each other all their lives. It just didn't seem possible.

While those thoughts were going through Bolo's brain, he didn't absorb what the lawyer was telling him. Sylvan was rambling on about how he should not talk to the police without him being present and about the conditions and requirements of bail.

"I had two FBI agents here," said Bolo. "They came as soon as I was well enough to talk with them."

"What did you tell them?

"They told me what I was charged with, and then they read me my rights. When they told me that I didn't have to answer questions without an attorney present, I told them I would prefer to wait. I didn't tell them anything. Why did it take you so long to get here?"

"I was undecided as to how best to represent you. Mr. Dilmore told me to represent Mitch. I started that process and I worried that there might be a conflict of interest for me to represent both of you. The charges against Mitch were more severe than those against you. His leadership role created that. I was planning to have another lawyer represent you when Mitch no longer needed me. I can now give you my full attention, that is if you want me. You could hire another lawyer or choose the public defender. It's up to you."

"You're the Boss's lawyer. I want you to handle my case."

"Good. Now you do understand that anything you tell me is privileged information and I am not required to share it with the prosecution. Do you understand that?"

"Yes, I'm good to go," said Bolo. "I just can't believe Mitch is gone. The FBI people led me to believe that he only had minor injuries and that he was already in jail."

"That is correct. I'm just as mystified as you. They're not telling me anything at this point. But my priority is you now."

The lawyer reached into his briefcase and pulled out a road atlas. He opened it up for Bolo to the Ohio page. He handed him a highlighter pen. He explained to Bolo that he needed information about the locations and route they travelled from the time they stopped at the farm in Pennsylvania until they reached Toledo. He then turned back to the Pennsylvania map page.

Bolo was able to pinpoint the location of his cousin, Richard Fleming's home. From there he could trace the route to the farm. He highlighted the route they took getting there from I-79 also.

Bolo gave the attorney as much detail as he could remember about the farm and its residents, the Grants. He was able to draw a rough map of the layout of the buildings relative to the road and the fields. His detail of the inside of the barn was brief, having been inside only once. His memory of the inside of the house was good.

The attorney took notes as Bolo talked, interrupting with questions at times. They came up with an accurate drawing of the main floor plan of the Grant house.

Attorney Sylvan shifted the emphasis to the route taken from Fleming's house and through Ohio to Toledo. He had Bolo tell of each time they stopped, whether it was for fuel or for a restroom. Sylvan questioned why they left the interstate and went on to state Route 4.

"The cops had a roadblock set up to stop us at a rest area just before that exit. We were able to break through that and escape by going onto Route 4."

When Bolo showed the back-traced route in the area where they ditched the white van, the Attorney questioned that.

"That's where we switched cars," said Bolo. "The white van was too easy to spot. We grabbed the Pacifica at a car lot back in Bellevue. The place where we ditched the van was near this area called Flat Rock Park."

Bolo traced the remaining route to the Toledo city limits. When he had completed that, he pointed out where Mitch recognized that they had a tail behind them. They didn't know where they picked him up, but the blue Chrysler was following them. They tried a diversion through a warehouse complex. They thought it had been successful, but somehow the guy must have picked them up again. Suddenly he was behind them when they drove into the Boss's warehouse.

The attorney had Bolo give him as much detail as he could remember of what happened then. This was a critical part of the story. Dinny died here, Bolo was wounded, and Mitch was injured. Attorney Sylvan didn't want to be surprised by what would come later in a courtroom.

The attorney was pleased with what he had learned from his client. He had one more question.

"Bolo, what happened to the zip-drive?" he asked.

"What do you mean," he answered. "I don't know what you're talking about."

"One of these," he said as he opened his hand and showed one to Bolo. He suspected that his client might not be computer-literate, so he had brought one with him. "It's a memory stick that fits into a computer."

"If Mitch had one, I don't know about it. I don't own a computer. I always got Mitch to help me if I needed one for any reason."

"He would have picked it up in DC before you left for your return trip. He may have hidden it. It's small and should be easy to hide. Do you have any thoughts on that?"

"Maybe he just carried it in his pocket."

"They didn't find it on him, nor in his luggage or gear. They practically tore the car apart looking for it, but no luck."

"Is it important?" asked Bolo.

"It is," said the lawyer. "Mitch attended meetings at the hotel while you were there. This drive contained information about those meetings that could be harmful to everyone in the organization, including you. We need to find it. We need to find it before the police do."

Bolo thought long and hard about this before he finally responded.

"Mitch was anal about security. If it was that important, then he hid it, and he hid it well. The only place where it might be that you haven't mentioned being searched would be the white van. Mitch was under a lot of pressure when we did the switch. We transferred all our gear and wiped the van down before we abandoned it. He could have hidden something that small in an alcove somewhere in it and just, plain forgotten about it. I can't see him hiding it at the farm. That would have been too risky for him to do."

"You may have something there," said Attorney Sylvan. "I'll follow up on that. In the meantime, I'll set up a time we can get some preliminary questions out of the way with the FBI. We're not going to give them any more than we have to. I'll also work on getting you a bail hearing. Keep the faith."

Bolo was relieved to have begun his legal process. He felt confident that he had a good lawyer working for him. What bothered him now was what might be on the zip-drive. He had no idea what kind of trouble that might bring. He also couldn't help but wonder what happened to Mitch.

CHAPTER 84

Karen had John swing around to the back of the house.

"Only strangers use the front door here," she said. "Most farm homes are set up that way."

As the back porch recess came into view, Karen brought both hands up to her face and responded to what she saw.

"Oh my God," she said.

John stopped the car and looked at what she was seeing. Stretched across the top of the alcove was a computer-generated banner that read, 'Welcome Home Aunt Karen.' It was decorated with crayon-drawn additions that were obviously contributed by her young niece and nephew.

When Karen and John got out of the car, they were immediately surrounded by the Grant family. Martha, Kurt, Sheila, and the two children were there to bestow Grant hugs to Karen and John. Kurt introduced John to Sheila, 5-year-old Bobby and 3-year-old Nancy. After that, Martha ushered all of them inside to the kitchen.

They entered the kitchen and were immediately taken aback by another banner, stretched across the dining-room archway. This one was similarly decorated and said, 'Thank you John.'

If John had any doubts about how he would be accepted by the Grant family, they were now gone. He and Karen were ushered into the living room and seated together on the sofa.

Almost immediately, the two children filled the remaining space on the sofa. They told Karen and John about their experiences with the banners, about school, and any number of other things important to them.

"They're still excited about being reunited with their Dad," said Sheila. "The quarantine was over today. This is a special day for all of us."

After they all talked for a while, Martha announced that there was just enough time for the chores before dinner would be ready.

"Sheila and I have a special dinner planned for your welcome-home party," said Martha. "She will work with me on that while Kurt does the milking. Jake will be looking forward to seeing John and Karen, so the two of you can feed him. Bobby and Nancy can feed the chickens and gather eggs."

As they left the living room and donned work jackets and boots, John marveled at how similar farm life was to the military. Everyone had a job and there was a sergeant to dish out the orders. Kurt found work boots for John and Karen, and they all headed for the barn.

Daisy met them at her appointed time and Kurt and his pail followed her to the milking stall. John was concerned about the small children being able to perform their duty. What he saw was Bobby helping his little sister feed the chickens, while he began to gather eggs. As he and Karen watched, little Nancy had a smile on her face. She had obviously done this before.

John and Karen went to the upper level to feed Jake. As she measured out his feed she said, "You can feed him. It will help the two of you get reacquainted."

Jake dived right into his oats as soon as John reached in with the scoop. Then, without apparent reason he stopped and nuzzled John's hand.

"I think he remembers me," said John.

"Don't let it go to your head," said Karen. "He probably associates you with the amount of oats you gave him that day."

"Whatever it takes," said John. "I want to be his friend."

When they started back to the house, the children had finished their chores, and Kurt was just coming out of the lower level with his pail of milk. Bobby usually carried both containers of eggs, but Nancy insisted on carrying one. It was obvious that she needed to be more of a contributing factor. Unfortunately, at her age she was not steady enough to be sure that all the eggs would survive the journey to the house.

John sensed a conflict in the making and quickly asked Nancy if she would let him help her carry her pail of eggs. She was pleased with that, and the two of them walked side by side with John stooped to Nancy's level all the way to the house. Not an egg broke.

"How's your back, John?" asked Kurt.

"I'm fine," he answered. "I seem to remember doing a similar maneuver in basic training."

By the time they had removed their work gear and washed up, Sheila announced that dinner was served.

What John saw was unlike anything he had ever experienced. At home with his mother, it was rare that there were other people at dinner. Even in the officer's mess it was only on special holidays that anything came close to a meal presentation like this.

There was a roast chicken, along with all the usual side dishes one would expect at a Thanksgiving dinner. In addition to that was what appeared to be a rolled-rump roast of beef.

"Martha," said John. "There are *two* meals here. You went to a lot of trouble."

"I wasn't sure if you would like chicken," she answered. "I figured you would like our beef. Jake helped provide that, indirectly of course."

They all laughed at that. Even the children laughed. It was doubtful, however that they understood the humor of it.

Before they broke bread, they all joined hands around the table while Kurt said a special thanks and blessing for the occasion. John added a silent prayer of his own. He was thankful to be a part of everything that had transpired and caused him to be with this family today.

John marveled at how the conversation seemed to blend well among the three generations at the table. This was the first real experience he had of interacting with children since he was a child himself. Just when he felt he could eat no more, Martha went to the kitchen and returned with two pies.

"We have apple, made with two kinds of apples from our spring house storage. We have blackberry, made with berries from our thornless bushes along the path to the barn and from wild bushes along the woods line. What would you like, John?" she asked."

"Yes," answered John.

Martha got the message and served him a slice of each. She went around the table, asking each person what they would like. When she got to Bobby he said, "Yes."

Bobby got his two slices and John got credit for being a good teacher.

After they had all finished, John praised the cooks and especially the pies.

"How did you do the special roll around the crust edge?" asked John.

"That's a family tradition. I don't know where it started," said Martha. I know my grandmother did it, and I taught Karen when she was a young girl. Now Sheila does it too."

John looked at Karen and thought, *If I get this woman, I'll have to watch my waistline.*

Karen blushed. As usual she had read John's mind.

CHAPTER 85

Mitch regained consciousness. His condition had been upgraded from 'critical' to 'serious.' He was still a little groggy, but the nurse allowed his two visitors into the room.

"Welcome back," said Agent Stewell. "We almost lost you, but you came through the surgery and you're on the road to recovery."

"Yes, welcome back," said Agent Palmori.

Mitch was quiet for a while as he took in his surroundings and processed what he was seeing and hearing. The surgeon who had operated on him had checked on him in Recovery, but other than him only one nurse was there when he regained consciousness. He knew he had a pain in his side that got worse when he tried to move, but other than that he had no idea what was happening.

"How did I get here?" asked Mitch. "I was in the shower when a guy came in."

Mitch stopped abruptly as he remembered what happened. Some of the details were still hazy, but he was able to fill in the blanks.

"He tried to kill me. I was facing him when I was able to read his 'tell.' He spun me around, so my back was toward him. I thought he would either slit my throat or strangle me. I tried to lower myself to make it difficult for him. He was a big guy. I mean really big. He must have stabbed me, going for my heart. I don't know how I survived."

"You were lucky," said Connie. "A guard found you bleeding out. He and another guard, by their quick action got you medical attention. The knife just missed your heart."

"Did they catch the guy that did it?" asked Mitch.

"No." said Chick. "They saw him running away, and by his size they think they know who did it. Did you see him well enough to identify him?"

"I saw him well enough. I'll never forget him. In the shower like that, I never felt so vulnerable, or so scared."

"They'll want you to identify him by looking at some mug shots. If you can do that, it will be enough to get him charged. At this point we don't want to do a line-up. We don't want him to know that you survived. We'll be able to protect you better if it is reported that you are dead."

"How will you be able to keep the lid on that?" asked Mitch. "This is a public hospital. People come and go. Sooner or later, someone will finger me, and I'll be a target again."

"There is a 24-hour surveillance on your room, by select members of the local police force," said Connie. "The doctor attending you is one we have worked with before. There will be a minimal nursing staff, chosen for their ability to be discreet. When you can be discharged, which shouldn't be too long, you will be moved to a safehouse. Security there will be tight."

"I have some good news for you," said Chick. "We got it approved for you to enter the witness protection program, if you can supply the connection to your involvement in the rioting at the Capitol, and your involvement of its planning. Your greatest value to the investigation will be your ability to give testimony in any upcoming trial. In the interim, your protection and the secrecy of our mission will be vital to our success."

"How do you plan to keep me alive after I testify?" asked Mitch.

"We have teams who are expert in this," said Connie. "You would be given a new identity and moved to another part of the country. You should begin thinking about where you might like to live. I would suggest somewhere in a small town or rural environment in one of the fly-over states. We can place you in a job, or your age might allow you to receive a stipend, like a monthly retirement check. Those types of details will be worked out by your team."

"What about Bolo?" asked Mitch. "Can my deal include him?"

"It is always harder and riskier when more people are involved," said Chick. "Your ability and willingness to break ties with your current life will be entirely within your control if you go it alone. We already know that Bolo has a cousin that he maintains contact with. How many more relatives might there be? You obviously feel a responsibility toward him Are you sure he feels the same toward you? As the investigation plays out, we will have more knowledge of whether Bolo had any part in the attempt on your life. That attempt came as a result of knowledge someone had that they shouldn't have had. At this point we are not certain that Bolo is entirely innocent of helping those who want you removed from the case."

As Mitch contemplated all of this, Connie produced the document that would bind the deal for his cooperation. She explained it briefly to him and handed two copies to him for consideration.

"Take your time and read through this," she said. "You may want to have an attorney look at it. We would suggest that you choose a reputable lawyer, someone other than your Boss's attorney. We have determined that someone bugged your jail cell. Until we have more proof, we cannot comment further on that. It is important though, that we move quickly. The information you have is as much the target as you personally are."

As Connie went over this, Mitch remembered what the guy in the shower said right after he said he could keep his mouth shut. "That's not what I hear," the guy had said. Then he stabbed him.

Chick handed Mitch a card with private numbers for both the agents. "Call us if you have any questions, or if you need to have us come in again. Otherwise, we will call you if anything further develops that would be pertinent to your case. Get well. We hope to hear from you soon."

"Get well, Mitch," said Connie. "Do what's best for you."

CHAPTER 86

Nat McElhenny drove slowly by the state police barracks. It should be easy to spot what he was looking for if the information he had was good. Sure enough, there it was. The white van was in a compound behind the barracks. He went on down the road and turned. He drove by again, this time looking for how he might access the compound without being seen. There was a wooded area behind the compound. It separated the barracks lands from a housing plan. Just inside the woods line Nat spotted what he needed. An electrical sub-station with an access road from the housing plan would be perfect.

Nat drove into the sub-station area just at dusk. He parked behind the mass of the transformers and the enclosed utility building so that he could not be seen from the nearby houses. As he awaited total darkness, he went over his plan in his mind. He had placed the phony utility company signs on his van. He always carried generic coveralls with him when on a mission. He wore the proper company ball cap. A well-equipped tool belt finished his ensemble.

Nat carried an infrared tactical light to help him navigate through the woods area without falling over obstacles. All was quiet at the rear of the barracks building. His bolt-cutters made short work of the padlock on the compound gate. He slipped quickly inside. The door of the van was not locked. He opened it and quickly turned the headlight switch to the position that disabled the interior lights. Now he could open the door that had the armrest he was looking for. He tried a couple screwdrivers without success. Pressing hard, he was able to get the screw to move a little, but it was taking too long. He became frustrated and reached for his J-Bar pry bar. He forced the armrest completely off the door. Using his mini light, he inspected the back of the mounting, the door, and eventually the floor area to see if the drive might have fallen out without him noticing. No luck. Now he was starting to sweat. This was taking longer than he had planned. He hurried to the other side of the van, thinking that his information had been incorrect as to which door. He went right to the J-Bar this time and had the same result. The zip-drive was not there. Nat didn't like it but there was still one more thing he could do.

He went back to the prior location and opened the door again. He reached under the driver's seat and attached one of his bolt-head style bugs. He did a quick inspection of the floor areas where he had worked to be sure he hadn't left any tools behind, then beat a hasty retreat into the woods and back to his van.

CHAPTER 87

After dinner, John, Kurt and the children retired to the living room while the three women cleaned the table. The dishwasher made life easier from there on. Martha recalled that she didn't have that convenience when she raised her family. That coupled with the modernization of farming in general made farming much more desirable as an occupation.

As the ladies joined the others in the living room, Karen observed how John was slouched down on the sofa with his hands over his stomach.

"Don't worry, John," she said. "You'll work that off and then some tomorrow."

"I'll be thinking of you as I sit in my nice comfortable school bus," said Kurt. "I go back to the morning driving schedule tomorrow morning. I don't know how many students will be on the bus, or how I will deal with social distancing, but I'll have to deal with whatever it is."

"I have my regular hours at the bank," said Sheila. "They have been great with me when I had trouble getting a reliable sitter. That seems to be solved now, and between them, Kurt and Martha have filled in when needed."

"I go back to school," said Bobby.

"What do you do, Nancy?" asked John. "Everybody else seems to have important things to do. I was hoping you would be available to help me gather eggs."

"That's my job," said Martha. "Daisy has had her eye on you ever since you came here the first time. Karen will teach you how to milk Daisy. After that I'm sure she can find a few other things for you to do that will introduce you to farm life."

"What I have in mind for you will require a shovel," said Karen. "I'm guessing that you shoveled a lot of it to the enlisted men under your command in the Army."

"Did you have to clean out barns in the Army?" asked Bobby.

"That's what the Army is about," said John. "It's shoveled downhill. Somebody shovels it down to you and you shovel it down to the next guy. It all works out."

"What does the guy at the bottom of the hill do?" asked Bobby.

"He gets so much of it that he doesn't have time to worry about it," answered John.

"Bobby likes the Army," said Martha. "Do you think you still want to be in the Army?" she asked Bobby.

"I think I might switch to the Air Force, Grandma," he answered.

The rest of the evening passed that way, with the Grants getting to know John and vice versa. They all liked what they saw.

Kurt's family left for home first. They would have to rise early to get back to their regular routine.

Martha was next to call it a day. She said good night and told Karen and John what time breakfast would be.

"Do you mean we're going to eat *again*?" asked John.

"I'm sure you'll manage," said Karen as they said good night.

When they were in the privacy of their bedroom, John and Karen each reflected on the just completed day.

"You have a wonderful family, Karen," he said. "My life was nothing like what you have here. I had a sample of how other people lived on occasions when I visited with friends, but I never experienced anything like what you have here. I really like your family."

"I think you can see how they feel about you, John," she said. "You're a hero in their eyes. That's the way I feel about you too. In fact, that's only a small part of how I feel about you."

As they held each other in a comfortable embrace, Karen elaborated on her feelings about John.

"I've been thinking about our future together," she said. "I want to spend a couple of weeks here with Mom first. That will give Kurt a break and allow him to concentrate on his family for a while without the burden of the farm. After that, I would like to go back to Gainesville and resign my job at the hospital. If I work out a two week notice and leave on good terms, I will be able to get a nursing job just about anywhere in the country.

"If we drive back together, we could discuss our options as we travel. Once there we could live in my apartment. While I am at work you could look over the area and consider whether it holds any employment opportunities for you. If so, I would keep my job and we would live there until we get ourselves reestablished in Florida. If not, we could pack up my stuff, give up my apartment and head back here by way of Columbia. We could forward your Pods on to the farm. We could do what we're doing now, help Mom here at the farm, while you search out employment opportunities elsewhere. When you find a job you like, we can move on. 'Have nurse, will travel' as the expression goes. You'll have a hard time leaving without me."

"I wouldn't want any job that would require me to leave without you," said John. "That sounds like a good basic plan to me. Why don't we discuss it with Kurt and your Mom? If it works for everybody, we can plan to pull out in a couple of weeks."

They sealed it with a kiss and said goodnight.

CHAPTER 88

Sergeant McLaughlin got to his desk and was just getting into his morning routine when he got a 'squawk' from one of his patrolmen. As the man was making his rounds, inspecting the barracks' premises, he discovered the cut padlock on the gate to the compound.

"We had a visitor last night," he said. "The padlock to the compound has been cut. I haven't gone in yet."

"I'll be right out," said the Sergeant.

When he got there, he sent the patrolman into the compound and told him to see if he could find any evidence of tampering with any of the contents, or if anything was missing.

"I want to look at this van myself," he said.

After donning his gloves, he began to look at the van. The driver's door was not completely latched. When he opened it, he discovered that the interior lights did not come on. Seeing nothing out of place in the front area of the cab, he moved on to the next row seating area. He immediately found the dislodged armrests, one on each side. By the look of the interior door panels, the perp had used some sort of pry bar to remove the armrests. There was ripping at the edges of the screw holes. The Sergeant looked around the van interior and could find nothing else of interest.

While his patrolman was still occupied with his search of the compound, the Sergeant got out his cell phone and called John.

"I hope I didn't call too early, John," he said. "Someone broke into our compound last night. He went straight for the arm rests. He ripped them off from the inside door skins and left them lying on the floor. He apparently knew where to look and didn't bother anything else that I could see. Hold on a second, John."

The patrolman had finished his cursory search of the compound and reported back.

"I couldn't see that anything was missing," he said. "I found no evidence that anything was disturbed either."

"This is what he was after," said the Sergeant. "Get a 'crime scene' tape around the van and mark the lock for the fingerprint guys to check. Go ahead with your daily patrol. I'll wrap things up here."

"I'm back, John," he said. "I don't see how he would know you have the flash drive. Keep it in a safe place, just in case. Somebody must be worried about what's on it. I'll call you if anything else develops. Good luck milking the cow."

* * * * *

"Clear as a bell," thought Nat. "The bolt-head bug strikes again." Even though he could hear only one side of the conversation, it was enough. Nat had his friend Tim Patz develop the bug for him. Tim had field-tested it at an Elvis look-alike performance where they didn't allow recording devices inside the venue. Tim's wife Marge is an 'Elvis nut.' Nat reminded himself to buy something nice for Tim to give her.

Nat packed up his equipment and headed out of his surveillance spot. He always felt better when he put some distance between himself and the cops. His next thing to do was to call Jimmy Sylvan and report his findings. Jimmy wouldn't be happy about not recovering the drive, but Nat had the next best thing. He knew where it was, and Jimmy knew how to find the farm. After the call he would find some breakfast.

CHAPTER 89

Karen was in the shower when John got the call from Sergeant McLaughlin. He was startled to hear how fast things were moving. He decided to keep this latest revelation to himself for the time being. Karen and Martha deserved some worry-free time together.

John was the first to arrive at the kitchen, so he made use of that time to search out a small zip-lock sandwich bag. He took the flash drive from his pocket and sealed it in the bag. He had an idea of a safe place to put it. He would be able to accomplish that before the morning chores were completed.

Martha was next to arrive, followed within a few minutes by Karen. John was introduced to free-range eggs.

"I never would have realized that they would taste so much better," said John.

After breakfast, the three of them headed for the barn. Martha would get a break from dealing with the large animals, so she headed for the chicken coop. Judging from the racket they made, they were glad to see her.

Daisy's internal clock was working well as she ambled into the barn for the milking ritual.

"Why don't you feed Jake," said Karen "and I'll get Daisy her breakfast. We should be finished about the same time, so we can begin the milking lesson."

John headed up the ladder to the upper level and greeted Jake. He got his morning measure of oats and scooped it into his feed box. Jake was happy to see him, so John entered his enclosure and took advantage of the friendly welcome. He removed the baggie from his pocket and placed it on top of a horizontal beam that extended through the stall.

"Take good care of that Jake," he said. "I'll be back for it later."

John couldn't think of a safer place to hide the drive. He went back down the ladder and found Karen making final preparations for the milking process. She placed a three-legged milking stool in position and instructed John how to proceed.

"Daisy doesn't like cold hands," said Karen. "Rub her side a little before you start. That will help her get used to the temperature of your hands and help the two of you get acquainted. Next you clean all the area over the pail of any dirt or residue she might have picked up. What doesn't fall into the pail doesn't have to be removed later."

John could have made a comment at this point, but he didn't know how Karen might take it.

Karen went through a detailed explanation of grip, squeeze and pull as they pertained to the process. She demonstrated each for John. When he tried it, somehow it didn't work as well for him.

"It's not as easy as it looks," said John. "Daisy doesn't seem to mind my fumbling though. She just keeps munching away at her breakfast."

"It's a little awkward for everyone at first," she said, as she demonstrated where John could improve his technique.

John tried again and had a marked improvement.

"I do believe he's got it," said Karen. "What do you think Daisy? I think he might be a natural."

Just then Daisy let out a contented "Moo," and everyone was happy.

Karen showed John how to finish the process. Then they put some hay into the stall and went out to check on Martha. They found her finished with the chickens and egg gathering. She was just finishing a cell phone conversation.

"I was talking with Jose' Cantina," she said. "I invited him to have lunch with us. He's anxious to meet John. I told him to invite Trooper Weaver too, if he's able to get away."

"I hope they can both make it," said John. "They wrapped things up here right away by taking the Russians off our hands. It would be nice to meet them."

"That'll be great," said Karen. "I knew Jose' when we were in school. His sister was in my class. We were good friends. Jose' was a bit of a clown in those days. I wonder if his job has changed him very much. He was known for testing our olfactory senses. He'd let one go almost anywhere, then laugh about it. His explanation was that his family ate a lot of beans. Somehow, his sister didn't seem to have the same reactions."

"I know I'm going to like him. He would have fit in well in the military. Our food seemed to have similar effects," said John.

"We try to avoid foods that produce methane gas," said Martha. "We have enough of that around the cattle. We don't need any more in the house."

John took that as a subtle hint that he should behave himself around her. Karen confirmed his thoughts with a look.

"I was surprised to learn though," said Martha, "that there is now a market for manure for a process that extracts the methane for commercial use. It is treated and introduced into the standard gas lines. There is a company in Indiana County considering building a facility to do the process. The residue can be returned to the farm in a dried state for use as fertilizer. Kurt was approached by their representative about providing product from our cattle. It sounds like it would be a good thing for us. We have a natural gas well on the farm that has provided heat for the house for years. We get a small check periodically as a share of the production revenue."

"I've heard about the 'free gas' some people have in Pennsylvania and Ohio, as well as other areas," said John. "How does that work?"

Martha and Karen walked John through the natural gas drilling process and its effect on the landowners. They explained its history and, also its future possibilities.

"It sounds like a good deal for everybody," said John. "Why isn't there more deep-well drilling?"

"It's a hot potato," said Martha. "The environmentalists fear that fracking of the wells will harm the environment. They accuse the oil companies and landowners of 'greed.' The science of it all shows a forward path to prosperity, however, for every winner there is a loser. Politically it's a nightmare. One hopes that through education and understanding of each other's issues it will eventually work itself out."

"I have faith in our country to solve such problems," said John. "History shows us that our system of government always overcomes issues when the goal is good for the country."

"I hope you're right," said Martha. "We'll soon find out if our new president will continue with progress that has been made or will follow the path the socialists have marked out for him. I'm concerned. Meanwhile, let's get the milk and eggs processed so we can move on to what comes next."

"I guess I have more questions than little Bobby," said John.

"Not more, just more difficult to answer," said Karen. "It's how you boys learn."

The three of them chatted and became better acquainted as they completed the morning work. Martha and Karen switched to preparing lunch when the time came. They learned that they would have both police guests as they had hoped. Each arrived in one of his agency's cruisers. They parked behind the house so the neighbors wouldn't think another big arrest was happening.

After introductions were made, they all enjoyed a light lunch prepared by the Grant women. They learned that Trooper Weaver's first name was 'Michael,' but his friends called him 'Mikey.'

"The next time you visit I'll make you some traditional police food," said Martha.

"What might that be?" asked Mikey.

"Donuts, of course," said Karen.

While Karen and Martha cleaned up after lunch, John had an opportunity for a private conversation with the guests. He told Jose' and Mikey about the break in where the van was impounded, and the significance of what the perps were looking for. He asked Mikey to keep an eye on the farm during patrols in the area for the next several days, just as a precaution. He felt they were dealing with a sophisticated adversary, with surprisingly good resources.

After lunch, Karen and Jose' showed Mikey and John the Grant shooting range. Jose' had used the range many times, but the state police had their own facility. For long range, there was a bench rest and target stations at 100 yards and 150 yards. The pistol range had a covered station with target areas at 25 feet, 50 feet and 50 yards. The target areas were backed up by earthen embankments for safety. There was also an embankment between the range and the lower elevation house and barn areas. This helped with sound deadening and gave the range an element of privacy. To top it all off, the range had an old-fashioned outhouse. Karen offered Mikey the use of the range if he wanted to sneak in a little extra practice.

"That would be great," said Mikey. "With the pandemic we have had to forgo our regular range routines. The indoor facility we use is privately owned, and we must comply with their ideas of social distancing, masks, etc. The barracks has a contract with them for range time, but lately we have had a hard time getting accommodated. Besides a higher demand for shooting, they have had to deal with difficult market conditions."

"What do you mean?" asked John.

"They're having a hard time getting guns for their store," said Mikey. "Customer demand is off the charts. As soon as they get a gun into their inventory and available for sale, it is gone, often the same day. Then there is the problem of ammo shortage. Most stores hold back some, and don't sell all of what they have. They need to have enough on hand to sell with the gun. I've seen cases where the customer had to come back weeks later to get enough ammo to practice with his gun. It's crazy."

"I guess I've been out of touch," said John. "In the military we always had more than enough ammo. As a civilian it looks like I might have to resort to banging the bad guys over the head with my empty gun."

"It's not quite that bad," said Karen. "When the police use our range, they usually provide us with a 'tip' in the form of ammo. They also are well supplied."

Their law enforcement friends could access the shooting range by turning off the township road into the Grant driveway. Instead of following the driveway around behind the house, they would continue driving forward behind the garage and machine shed. That was an access into the fields, that also led to the range. If they parked in a designated area near the range their vehicles could not be seen from the township road.

"We put in the private parking area when we built the range," said Karen. "We didn't want those travelling the township road to see police cars parked at the house when the range was being used."

"I get it," said John. "No use fostering the rumor that those terrible Grants were involved in some sort of criminal activity."

"That would be reason enough," said Karen. "Our main concern was the privacy. There are people today that don't believe in private citizens ownership of firearms. We strongly support the second amendment. We just don't flaunt it."

After the two guests left, Karen took John for a walk around the parts of the farm he had not yet seen. She explained how each field was rotated for maximum crop production. He learned how the fields were drained to eliminate wet spots. He saw a few groundhog holes where the bravest of the little animals dared to encroach on the Grant farm.

"We hunt them from mid-summer until early October," said Karen. They can be destructive to the fields and can cause a hazard to the equipment."

"Why do you wait that long?" asked John.

"Let's call it the 'Geneva Convention' for groundhogs," said Karen. "If we shoot the mother while the babies are still unable to survive on their own outside the burrow, that is considered 'cruelty.' We wait until they are at least healthy teenagers before we pop them."

When they got back to the house, they found Martha ready for them. The three of them planned out some of the chores that needed to be done over the next few days. The weather was cooperating, and she wanted to give Kurt some time with his family while John and Karen were there to help on the farm.

While she and John were walking the fields, Karen had seen where some fences needed mending, and where some of the drainage system needed attention. She suggested that they work on those projects after their morning chores. Martha would then have time to catch up on some housework. When they had a rough plan in place for the next day, they settled in for an evening of rest and conversation.

Martha was still curious about the events that took place during the time Karen was held captive and how she was rescued. John had held back some of the details when he talked with Martha and Kurt. He didn't want to worry them needlessly. Now that Karen was back and unharmed, they deserved the unvarnished truth of the ordeal. The family could be proud of how well she handled herself. Many people would have taken months, maybe even years to return to normal. John was also proud of Karen. As he related the detail of what had taken place during the kidnapping, he took the opportunity of the conversation to tell Martha what a great daughter she had. They all felt closer, more like a family, when they retired for the night.

CHAPTER 90

Mitch made the call to Agent Stewell. He had given the matter a lot of thought, and he concluded that what they offered him was the best deal he was going to get. He waived his right to have an attorney look over the documents. He understood everything, and he had come to trust the two agents.

His doctor had just told him that his wound was healing well, and he could expect to be discharged in a couple of days. He had been thinking about where he might like to be relocated, but he had not yet decided on a place.

Agents Stewell and Palmori arrived at 3 PM with documents in hand and with a notary to make the signatures legal and proper. After going over everything one more time, they all signed and made it official. Mitch now had a new life.

Mitch stopped the Agents as they were about to leave and asked where they had in mind for him to be relocated.

"We don't know, and we won't know," said Agent Palmori. "That's between you and your contact person within the program. We won't even see you again except maybe at a trial where you would be a witness. Even in that case, you would be brought to us, and we still wouldn't know where you were located. The program representative will be in contact with you very soon to work out details with you."

"Agent Palmori and I both feel that you have an excellent chance for success in this program, Mr. Mitchell. We thank you for your cooperation in the case, and we wish you the best in your new life."

They went out the door and out of Mitch's life. One hour later he had a visit from his program representative. After a lengthy conversation, Mitch learned that he would be relocated to a small midwestern town where he would have the opportunity to take a job as a property manager, something he knew how to do. Given his age, he could opt for a small retirement stipend in lieu of the job. Mitch didn't hesitate about that option. He took the job.

His representative arranged to pick him up when he was discharged and accompany him to his new location and help him get settled into his new life. Mitch was having a good day.

CHAPTER 91

Jimmy Sylvan formed a tent with his fingers, a sign that he was deep in thought. Seated across his desk from him was his principal client, Wade Dilmore. Jimmy was being asked to do something that stretched beyond the bounds of ethical legal practice. He had represented Dilmore for many years and had often walked a line that some would say was dangerous to his reputation. In these instances, he had always felt that he was in control of the situations. The risks were minimal, and the rewards were great. Dilmore had brought a lot of money into Jimmy's legal practice.

What he was being asked to do this time scared him. He had never gone this far astray before. Dilmore had always managed his businesses with an element of control that Jimmy was comfortable with. This time was different, however. This time there was a powerful unknown quantity pulling the strings. Not only was the power outside of Jimmy's control, but it was also outside of Dilmore's.

"All I want you to do is go along for the ride," said Dilmore. "You don't have to get involved in anything outside of your comfort level. I Just need you there to represent my interests. I can't be sure the others don't plan to throw me under the bus. I don't want to be the fall guy if things don't go as planned."

"I'm not a 'boots on the ground' person Wade," said Sylvan. "My job is to represent you 'legally'. I can't do that very well with my feet stuck in the mud. I suggest we get McElhenny to go. He has really come through for you so far. For the right price, he will do it again."

Dilmore thought about this for a while, then responded.

"They're not using any of my men for this," he said. "That worries me. It looks to me like they don't want to be hampered by having to protect my interests. In one way, that's good for them. In another way, it gives me an opportunity for plausible deniability. I just need to be sure I come out clean."

After some additional thought, Dilmore came up with a workable plan.

"I want McElhenny in an untraceable vehicle. He can ditch it if it becomes necessary. His own vehicle will be stashed somewhere within walking distance of where he ditches the other one. If things go bad, he can get away clean and report back to you with the details."

"That should work," said Sylvan. "With Mitch out of the picture, that flash drive becomes all-important. With it in our possession, we are home free. Without it, we begin working on a Plan-B. Even that will be easier if you are kept clear of whatever happens at the farm."

"Tell McElhenny it will be his usual fee if things go as planned and the drive is recovered. If things get heavy-handed and he can keep me from being involved, he will get double his usual amount."

"He'll like that," said Sylvan. "I'll get working on it."

"I'll come up with a reasonable explanation for his presence on the mission. I can handle that."

CHAPTER 92

Martha was busy in the kitchen when John and Karen came in for breakfast.

"That looks like donuts you're making Mom," said Karen. "Does that mean we're having company for lunch?"

"It does," she answered. "I just got a text from Jose'. He and Mikey are coming to use the range today. There will be one additional man from the barracks today. They will arrive after lunch, so I am making dessert. You and John should plan on only a half-day of chores so you can join them on the range. Jose' wants to see who is the better shot, you or John."

"Are you going to shoot too?" asked Karen.

"Not this time," she answered. "I have some meat thawed, and I had planned to do some cooking. Maybe next time. I'll challenge the winner."

At breakfast they talked about the family shooting skills. John began to feel that his military training may have been second-rate.

"Can you milk Daisy after you feed Jake?" asked Karen. "I will feed the chickens and deal with the egg and milk processing."

"I can manage that," said John. "Will you want me to help you carry the eggs?" he asked Karen.

"I wouldn't want Nancy to get jealous," she answered. "Grant women can become violent when they get jealous."

Martha just smiled at the budding romance as John and Karen headed for the barn.

John found Jake to be his usual hungry self. Daisy was a pleasant surprise for him. She responded well to his apprentice milking skills. It may have been his imagination, but he thought she was whispering muffled 'mruphs' and 'gloptshes' to him as she enjoyed her breakfast. He would have to ask Karen for a translation of 'cow talk'.

He went back to the house with his pail of milk and found Karen and Martha busy with the eggs. He offered to strain the milk for them. Martha broke away from egg detail and instructed John on how to accomplish that.

"You're becoming quite the farmer John," said Martha. "I suppose you'll be wanting to drive the tractor next."

Karen laughed. "That's exactly what I was going to have him do," she said. "I want to take some posts out to the fields and get them ready for fence repair tomorrow. That should be a good half-day job for us to do before lunch and the big shooting match."

"I see what you're up to now," said John. "You're trying to wear me down, so I won't be steady enough for a good performance on the range."

"Maybe you'd rather help Mom with the cooking," she offered. "Of course, there's the risk that you might burn your trigger finger."

"The risk would be for those who might eat my cooking," said John. "I'd better stick with the fence posts."

"Honestly," said Martha. "You two go on like an old married couple."

"That observation might be closer to the mark than you think," said John.

They all smiled at what John said and continued working quietly with their duties.

When they had finished and Karen and John left for their planned work, Martha texted a message to Jose'. She suggested that the police group go directly to the range and begin practicing. Karen and John would be joining them. All were to come to the house for donuts afterwards.

"The tractor is an older John Deere," said Karen. "Kurt prefers an older model of this brand because it is user friendly. Many of the newer models are designed such that they are difficult to work on for a backyard mechanic. This is fine for a larger farming operation, but for a one tractor farm like ours, simpler is better. Kurt loves this old machine."

With that, Karen climbed up into the seat and started the tractor. She backed it expertly out of the machine shed, turned it around, and positioned it for hooking up a small flat-bed trailer.

She had John take over the driving duties while she directed him to a stack of fence posts for loading onto the trailer. John proceeded to back the trailer into just the right position for loading.

"Where did you learn how to do that?" she asked. Karen was surprised that he knew how to back a trailer.

"The Army taught us how to do a few things," he answered. "I never learned how to milk a cow, but if circumstances had been just slightly different, I once nearly had to milk a goat."

"I'd like to hear that story," said Karen.

"Let's save that for another time," he said.

They finished loading enough posts for repairs to the determined areas of the fences. John pulled out with the load. Karen stood farmer style on the axle with her arm around John for support.

They spent the balance of the morning delivering the posts around the farm to the places where the fences needed repairs. John came to appreciate how Karen achieved her muscular build. She looked like a woman, an extremely attractive woman, but she had strength that surpassed many men.

When they had delivered all the posts, they headed back to the house with the trailer.

"Park it behind the house," said Karen. "We can load up our shooting supplies after lunch and drive them up to the range."

They went into the kitchen and found Martha, as usual, one step ahead of them with a prepared lunch. By the time they washed up, they were ready to sit down to eat.

After lunch they all paid a visit to Martha's armory. Karen pulled a rifle from the gun safe and showed it to John.

"This is the rifle that both Kurt and I used in the small-bore competition when we were in high school. The NRA sponsored a local club that had a youth program. We had certified instructors, free ammunition, and a range at the club to use for our competitions. It's one of the few sports where males and females could participate on an equal footing. In my senior year, Kurt and I were on the same team. We were unbeatable that year."

"I'm familiar with the program," said John. "I didn't have the benefit of early training though. I remember that there were a couple of guys who were heads and tails above the rest of us on the rifle range in basic training. I was fortunate to have good instructors, but it still took me a while to catch up."

"Frank was interested in the shooting sports too," said Martha. "When the kids got involved is when he built the range. We were fortunate to have the land with a natural terrain that permitted a safe backdrop for shooting. Both of the kids were good, but they still couldn't top Frank for the shooting skills."

Martha chose a rifle for John. Then both he and Karen chose from the stock of handguns. They filled a canvas bag with ammo and their ear protection.

They loaded everything onto the trailer and were ready to head out. Martha wished them good luck and safe shooting as they headed for the range.

When they got there, they found Jose' already getting set up. He was in civilian clothes.

"This is my day off," he said. "The other guys are on duty and will not be able to stay long. At least they will be able to get familiar with the range. I'll be able to stay around and supervise the competition between you two hot shots. Jubila made me a good lunch today, so I'm in good form."

"I've heard about your shooting skills Jose'," said John. "I understand you're famous in some circles."

"I can thank Jubila for that," said Jose'. "Today she made a salad with black beans. They can give me that extra shooting skill. It should kick in about an hour from now."

Just then John's cell phone rang.

"Martha wants to speak to you," he said to Karen.

"What's up," she said as she took the phone.

"Okay, I have time to do that now," said Karen. "The state guys haven't arrived yet."

"Mom forgot to tell me that Dr. Nayar dropped off Jake's medicine this morning," she said.

"I didn't know Jake was ill," said John. "He looked like he was rearing to go when I fed him this morning."

"He is 'rearing to go' as you put it, but what he wants to go *after* is the herd of females in the pasture on the next hill. He gets vitamin shots, one per day, beginning today, for the next week. This will help him build up his stamina. Think of it as 'Viagra for bulls.' Kurt usually gives him the shots, but since I'm here I get the honors. I'll run down now and take care of that while you two set up the range."

Karen was nearly back to the barn when a state police cruiser pulled into the parking area with Mikey at the wheel. He was alone.

"Where's your partner"? asked Jose' "We were looking forward to giving you boys a lesson today."

"He got called out on a domestic at the other end of the county," said Mikey. "It'll be just me for the lesson."

Jose' and John explained Karen's absence to Mikey. The three of them enjoyed a bit of crude farm-boy humor at her expense. They soon got serious though and proceeded to hang targets on the range standards in preparation for the shooting.

Then John's phone rang again.

CHAPTER 93

Nat McElhenny was driving as part of a three-car convoy. He was elated when Sylvan had explained what was needed of him, and especially with what the job paid. He had some second thoughts when he met up with the others who were involved in the mission.

Nat had operated on the fringes of legality in his trade as a private investigator. He had met and associated with some of the lower elements of society. It came with the job. This group though, came closer to the bottom of the barrel than any he had previously encountered. Nat was worried.

The leader of the group rode in the first car with two other men. The second car also held three men. Nat had only one man riding with him. One of the men in each car had a rough-drawn topographical map of the farm. They also had a floor plan drawing of the house.

The leader of the gang communicated with the others by means of walkie-talkies. Nat's passenger held the device and sat quietly as they followed the other two cars.

It wasn't their appearance. They were dressed well enough. They were all clean-shaven. When they spoke, it was only with a purpose. There was no banter of a type one would expect from a group of men. It was something else. There was an intensity about them that was beyond natural. They didn't use names but referred to each other by means of a code of some sort. Their leader was called 'Secretary.' It all had an effect on Nat that made him feel like an outsider. Nat could see bulges in the jackets the men wore that indicated they were armed. He wouldn't be surprised if the first two cars contained additional weapons.

The walkie-talkie squawked and a message came through from the leader as the convoy slowed to a stop.

"We're here," he said. "The name on the mailbox is 'Grant.' Cars one and two will pull into the driveway and continue past the back of the house and stop between the house and barn. They will await further instructions. As we enter the driveway Mr. M will exit his vehicle and take a position behind the shed on the right side of the drive. Car three will not turn into the driveway but will continue along the township road till in the vicinity of the back of the barn. Find a place to pull off the road where you can observe the barn and cover us from that angle. Don't forget, this guy has taken out six men. Be careful."

As they started to move again, cars one and two made the turn to the driveway. Mr. M jumped out and ran to the back of the outbuilding as instructed. As the cars turned past the back of the house Nat moved forward toward the back of the barn. He spotted a clear area on his left just past the barn where he could pull off into a grove. He pulled into the open area and shut off his engine. There was a clear view of the back of the barn. His passenger reported that they were in position.

CHAPTER 94

As John took the call, his expression immediately turned serious. The others noticed it and were concerned. He waved them over closer to the phone so they could hear Karen's half of the conversation. They learned that she was in the upper level of the barn and safe for the moment. She had remembered to take her phone when she stopped at the house for Jake's medicine.

"Hang up and call your mother," said John. "Have her lock the doors, get to the second floor and make sure she is armed. She can watch out the windows at that level and see what is going on. She should beep you if she is in any danger. When you get that done, call me back. I'll be on vibrate mode."

While they were waiting for Karen's call, the men got their rifles locked and loaded. They made sure their handguns were at the ready. They were beginning to form a contingency plan when Karen's call came in.

"Mom has been alerted, and she is moving into action as you suggested," said Karen. "Wait! One of them is getting out of the car and walking toward the barn."

"Karen," said John. "Leave your phone on, but button it into your shirt pocket. That way we'll be able to hear you if you have to move quickly."

"He's getting closer," she said. "I have to hide."

Karen saw the guy slide the barn door open enough to slip through. He did not announce himself, but at least his hands were empty. He moved cautiously through the dimly lit area, unaware of what might be ahead of him. He reached into his jacket and came out with a semi-automatic handgun. He was probably concerned about a possible unknown human presence in the shadows. Little did he know that a pair of wide-set bovine eyes watched his every move.

Karen held her breath to further mask her presence.

"Just a little further," she thought as he inched past her hiding place.

Just when she felt confident that he was safely past her, Jake let out two very loud snorts. These were followed by some heavy pawing in the straw and some butting against the slatted walls.

The guy let out a yelp as he lurched backwards and nearly fell. Karen helped him with that as she stepped from the shadows and bashed him over the head with the same shovel John had used on the Russians.

A barn has certain identifiable odors. Karen was familiar with these, and what she smelled was not one of them.

"I think Jake scared the crap out of him," she said.

"Say again," whispered John.

Karen explained what had happened and told John she was in the process of using his hog-tying method to secure him. John told her there was no further activity at the cars. He also told her that Jose' had texted to her Mom, and that they now have a communications link.

Karen was greatly relieved at this news. She finished tying and gagging the guy. She covered him with hay and returned to her watching post.

"One down," she reported to John. "I relieved him of a very nice Glock-19."

"Good job," he responded. "While you were busy with that guy, Mikey took the opportunity to call in back-up. We weren't sure what they were about until your guy tipped their hand. He also had the barracks contact Todd at Homeland Security. They will probably be interested in talking with these guys."

"Someone's getting out of the first car again," said Karen.

The man stood by the door of his car and yelled toward the barn.

"Mr. B," he said. "Report."

He got no response, then repeated his words, only louder this time. After the third try he apparently gave up and reached into the car. He came out with a bullhorn and made an announcement with it.

"John Osmond," he said. "Come out. We want to talk to you." He waited a while then made that announcement again, with this added comment. "We just want to talk."

John waited a few seconds, then he walked to the top of the rise, where he would be visible from the farmyard. He carried his rifle.

"Are you looking for me?" he shouted. "I'm John Osmond. What is it you want?"

"You have something we want," said the spokesman.

"What might that be?" asked John.

"The flash-drive," he said. "You have it and it doesn't belong to you. We came here to take it off your hands. I'm giving you a chance to avoid trouble."

"That sounds fair," said John. "I'll give you an equal chance to avoid trouble. Turn your cars around and leave this property, immediately."

"What about my man that went into your barn?" he asked. "We can't leave without him. He might have fallen and hurt himself."

"He might have," said John. "Leave your address and we'll send him to you."

Just then the man made an unusual motion with his arm. John knew what was coming and he dived for the ground just as the shot rang out. It didn't feel like he had been hit, but sometimes that can be deceiving. While he was sorting that out, Jose' solved the riddle. He reported that the shot was from Martha. She saw a sniper taking a bead on John, and she took him out.

While John was occupied the two cars emptied out. Five armed men stood between their cars and the barn. They had a combination of rifles and shotguns.

Meanwhile, Jose' and Mikey had spread themselves apart from John along the top of the rise. They were in prone shooting positions and had a bead on the visitors below.

Mikey had his bullhorn handy, thinking he might be needing it.

"This is Trooper Weaver of the Pennsylvania State Police," he said. "Lay down your weapons and assume prone positions face down on the ground with your hands and feet spread apart. You are all under arrest."

With those words, their leader, apparently the 'chairman' took a position behind his car and fired a volley toward the top of the rise where he had seen John.

That became the signal for the good guys. Jose' and Mikey took out the tires on the near side of the two cars and placed a couple of shots into the side windows for effect. Then they switched to the old-west style of having the perps do a dance. Well placed shots near their feet had them going in circles. The one on the house end of the row broke in that direction, but Martha sent a volley that had him scurrying back to the group. The same thing happened when two of them tried a run for the barn. Karen had a full clip in the Glock and put most of those nineteen bullets into the ground in front of them.

When they had them corralled Mikey called for a 'cease fire' and it suddenly got quiet.

"Let's try that again," said Mikey. "The man leaning on the car roof will slide his weapon to the ground, then spread his hands reaching for the center of the roof. The rest of you will do what I told you to do the first time. Any failure to cooperate will result in the risk of serious bodily injury. Move now."

The four minions discarded their weapons without hesitation, but the leader looked from side to side from his position sprawled on the roof. He developed a disgusted look on his face as he too complied and slid his weapon to the ground.

* * * * *

When the shooting started, Nat's passenger lowered his side window and peered out as he listened to try and determine what was happening. When he was properly positioned, Nat reached his left hand down alongside his seat and retrieved his taser. He sent a dart into the body of his companion that immobilized him almost immediately. The guy gave him a look that would have killed, had he been able to accomplish that with his diminished nervous system.

Nat relieved him of his weapon and shoved him out the door. He knew where he was headed. He had stashed his van at the township fairgrounds. There were lots of buildings there that weren't being used this time of year. He had parked behind one of them. He had also spotted a place to ditch the car he was driving. He wiped it clean of his prints. He wasn't worried about his passenger's prints.

Once back on the road, he heard police sirens. They were probably headed for the farm. Being a good citizen, Nat pulled aside to give them plenty of room as they passed. Then he drove on and resumed his thoughts of how he would enjoy his newfound wealth.

CHAPTER 95

John and his two friends made their way down the slope toward the two disabled cars and the five captives. Karen had emerged from the barn and covered the men spread-eagled on the ground. She knew that they all probably had handguns under their coats, but they weren't in a position to get at them quickly. She hoped none of them tried anything because she only had two or three shots left in her gun.

While John and Jose' provided cover, Mikey began to search and cuff the men on the ground. He quickly ran out of handcuffs and had to finish the job with zip ties. He found that they all carried handguns, and two of them had backups strapped to their legs. One had a wicked looking skinning knife in a sheath attached to his belt.

"I assume that you gentlemen all have the proper permits for these weapons," he said.

He didn't get a response, so he began to read them their rights.

Karen and John left Mikey and Jose' to their duties and went to find Martha. She was on station at one of the upstairs windows that faced in the direction of the machine shed.

"Let's go check on the guy I shot," said Martha. "I don't want him to bleed out for lack of attention."

They made their way out to the wounded man. John was careful to keep him covered until he was sure the guy posed no threat. John relieved him of his weapons and the two women, always nurses first and foremost, began to examine his wound.

"It looks like you took out his kneecap," said Karen. "What happened here, Mom?" she asked.

"I was watching and listening with my window partially open. John was standing on the top of the rise. I could see this guy, but he didn't know I was watching. Suddenly he raised his rifle and began to take a bead on John. I couldn't very well let him shoot my future son-in-law," she said.

"Thank you for saving my life, Martha," said John. He gave Martha one of her signature 'Grant woman' hugs, but this time in reverse. Karen soon joined in and made it a group hug.

Karen returned to the larger group and asked Jose' to call for an ambulance. Just then the first contingent of state police arrived on the scene in the form of two patrol cars. Those officers began to help Mikey process the prisoners. They were followed closely by the barracks commander in another cruiser. He had a guy in the cage in the area behind the front row seats. He introduced himself as Lieutenant Long.

"I picked up this guy staggering on the road just across from the Grant barn," he said. "He was disoriented and didn't seem to be aware of much of anything. I could see through his open jacket that he wore a shoulder holster, but he had no gun. I figure he was somehow involved in what happened here. We'll question him when he is in better shape."

"Oh, I almost forgot," said Karen. "With everything happening so fast I didn't tell you about the one inside the barn."

Mikey detailed two officers to accompany Karen into the barn and relieve her of her prisoner. After a few minutes they had him untied and cuffed. They came out of the barn with him held between them.

"He's walking kind of funny Karen," said Jose' "What did you do to him?" (Jose' knew what had happened, but the situation became more humorous when Karen told it.)

"He had a little accident," said Karen. "He encountered Jake in the dark. Jake snorted and made some threatening moves. It apparently scared the crap out of him. I took him out of play with a shovel over the head. I wasn't about to clean him up. I've had enough of that sort of thing as a nurse. This probably falls under the jurisdiction of the police."

"I'll tell you one thing," said Lt. Long. "He's not riding in my cruiser. Rank has its privileges. Only in Bullskin Township could something like this happen."

One of the patrolmen relieved John and Martha from watching their prisoner. The ambulance arrived and they loaded him and left for the hospital. John and Martha came back to the group and were brought up to date.

They were just about to load up some of the prisoners when they were surprised by the noise of a low-flying helicopter.

"Look who's arriving late for the party," said John.

Todd Farley piloted the helicopter that landed in the field. With him were the two FBI agents.

"We were interviewing Sergeant McLaughlin about the break-in at his barracks when the call came in that you had visitors," said Todd. "It looks like you have things under control here."

John excused himself and went into the barn. He returned momentarily with the plastic bag containing the flash drive.

"This is what they were looking for," he said. "I had placed it in Jake's stall for safekeeping. Karen and I have listened to it already. She recognizes Mitchell's voice. If I'm not mistaken, this one is also on the recording." John indicated the leader of the group, the 'Secretary'.

"Who is Jake?" asked Todd.

"He is our 1000-pound bull, with an attitude," said Karen. "He's friendly with our family, and now with John. Even if they had known the drive was hidden in Jake's stall, it's certain they would have had a fight on their hands to get it."

"This is a rough looking team you were up against," said Agent Stewell. I'm anxious to learn how you prevailed."

"If you're keeping score," said John. "It's Grant Women-2 and Bad Guys-Zero."

Martha and Karen were beaming.

CHAPTER 96

THE NEXT DAY two tow-trucks came to the farm and hauled the two cars to the State Police impound lot. Their evidence techs would go over them to see what they could find.

After questioning the man that they found along the road, they determined that he was a part of the gang that invaded the farm. They got a break when the abandoned car No 3 was found near the township fairground complex. The man's fingerprints were found in the car. A local man tasked with the security of the complex had found the car. He also reported that a van had been parked behind one of the buildings in the afternoon of the day before. Unfortunately, he did not get a plate number.

Since two states were now involved in the investigation, the FBI took over the interrogation of the prisoners. After they questioned several of the minions, they had testimony pointing to the one called 'Secretary.'

The man refused to give his name. In fact, he refused to talk at all. A check of his fingerprints revealed that he had been in the military, albeit for only a short time. He was released on a bad-conduct discharge in 1971. His name was Donald Bevins. His current residence was Las Vegas. Mr. Bevins had served time for a variety of reasons, the most serious of which was embezzlement. There was no record of any current source of income.

Agent Palmori recited his name and much of his criminal record.

"Does any of that ring any bells for you Mr. Bevins?" she asked. "You may have wanted to keep your name secret from your associates, but thanks to your fingerprints, we now know a lot about you."

"You don't know anything," said Bevins.

"Suppose I told you that we have listened to the recorded voices on the flash drive. What a strange meeting. I want to thank you for the few words you just spoke. They will provide us with enough of a sample to compare your voice to one of the speakers on the recording."

Bevins started to squirm in his seat. Beads of perspiration came out on his forehead. After what seemed an eternity, he finally spoke.

"Okay, so what do you want from me?" he asked.

"For starters," said Palmori, "we want the names of the other people on the recording."

"It was all in code," he said. "We weren't supposed to know each other's names."

"We figured that," said Agent Stewell. "We also figure that you were the one person in the room that knew everyone's name. You were the Secretary."

There was another long pause from Bevins before he spoke again.

"I'm a dead man," he said. "It was my job to keep a record of the meeting. The flash drive was supposed to be encrypted. I just forgot to do it. I wasn't sure. That's why I had to get it back. All of us were wound up with the importance of the mission. There were a lot of details to plan."

With that, he leaned over in his chair and held his head in his hands.

"Will you be able to keep me alive?" he asked. "I'll tell you everything I can if you protect me."

"We'll have to take this to our supervisor Mr. Bevins, but I'm confident he will agree to that," said Stewell.

* * * * *

Todd Farley called and arranged to meet with the Grants at 3 PM. Mikey drove him to the farm in an unmarked car.

The news media had become aware of the excitement at the Grant farm and had showed up on their doorstep early that morning. They didn't spend a lot of time there since Martha, Karen and John were somewhat tight-lipped about all of it. They preferred to have any news releases come from the police or the FBI. Besides that, the reporters had to follow them to the barn and pose their questions during the regular farm routines.

Karen and John put off their fence repairs for another time. Martha busied herself in the house until Mikey and Todd arrived. She would have normally had something to offer as the hostess, but she didn't have to worry about that. With all the excitement yesterday, she had completely forgotten about the donuts. She would serve those and still have plenty left for the freezer.

Todd brought them up to date on the progress that had been made in the investigation. He told them that the FBI agents had been able to get the leader to cooperate. They were hopeful that his information would lead to more arrests, and more answers about the riot at the Capitol. They also found a couple of the minions eager to cooperate.

"You three, along with Jose' scared the bejabbers out of them," said Todd. They think you are all a bunch of overzealous cowboys. They will probably be happy to return to their respective crime-laden cities."

Sergeant McLaughlin sent his best regards to Karen and John. He had passed the original flash drive on to Todd yesterday so that a chain of custody could be preserved.

"I'm glad we got that original," said Todd. "I wouldn't want to have to explain Jake as part of the chain of custody for your copy."

"Jake has plenty of experience influencing judges at the fairgrounds," said Karen. "He would probably have made a good impression."

"I don't know how far up the chain of responsibility we will be able to take this," said Todd. "If we're lucky, we will find out who the 'Chairman' is. The tough one will be 'the money man.' If that trail goes far enough into the seats of power in our government, sometimes we cannot take things to a satisfactory conclusion. That's one of the frustrations of my job."

"It would seem to me that Karen and I are no longer at risk from these people," said John.

"I agree with you," said Todd. "The only one that would worry about you now would be Wade Dilmore. His organization is still on the hook for kidnapping charges. Right now, he would probably be happy to have you out of the picture, but soon that will change. We will have Mitch's cooperation. His testimony will be enough to close the book on all of that."

John and Karen gave puzzled looks at one another.

"I thought Mitch was dead," said Karen.

"He almost was, but he survived. We have him under wraps. He has agreed to provide what we need to tie Dilmore into the conspiracy for the Capitol riots. He can also close the books on a lot of local crime where he was involved with Dilmore through the years."

Todd wanted to meet Jake, before he and Mikey left. Karen even took a picture of him with Jake, and made it look like a 'selfie' for Todd to show to his friends at work. Jake seemed pleased with all of it.

Mikey drove Todd back to his helicopter where they met the FBI agents. They left with a good supply of donuts.

EPILOGUE

TWO WEEKS LATER things were getting back to normal.

The cases were progressing. Additional arrests were made. Chief Tallman was pleased that some open cases in his jurisdiction and in surrounding locales were being cleared. Reward money from two bank robberies was released and forwarded to John. He was thrilled. The first thing he did was pay Martha back the money she provided when he went on the rescue mission for Karen.

They still were holding on to the two guns that belonged to Martha. They would be needed for evidence in the upcoming trials. There was no hurry there, as Martha had more guns than she needed.

Karen had completed the regimen of vitamin shots for Jake. He was happily making the rounds of the females that were scheduled for breeding.

John and Karen completed many of the list of chores that was always demanding attention at a farm. Kurt would be returning to his normal farm routine on the following Monday. Martha was looking forward to seeing more of her grandchildren.

Several days ago, Karen had gone into Greensburg to Excela's Westmoreland Hospital. She got a job application and was granted an immediate interview. Excela has three hospitals in their system, all within driving distance of the farm. She has a job waiting for her if she wants it.

John has been thinking more and more about a law enforcement career. With his background, he would qualify for entrance into several federal agencies, as well as to the state or local police forces. He would decide which way he wanted to apply once he and Karen made the decision where they wanted to live.

Karen and John were packed for their trip to Florida. They were having a family dinner that evening and leaving early the next day. They planned to follow the ideas Karen had for evolving into their future together.

When they got to South Carolina, where John's belongings were stored, he wanted to retrieve a few things. First and foremost, would be his mother's wedding and engagement rings. He planned to put the latter in a more appropriate place.

The End

John Osmond left the Army as a Captain. Being a Green Beret, he had seen action in remote corners of the globe. Karen Grant was a charge nurse at a Florida hospital. She was headed north to help with a family emergency in western Pennsylvania. John was headed north to check out a job prospect in western New York. Fate brings the two together while enroute. Six men who participated in the Capitol riot forced themselves into the family farm where Karen's mother lived. After a text from her brother alerts her to the situation, John insists on helping Karen. When they reached the farm, they began to spoil the plans of Mitch, the leader of the invaders. What happens next took them all on a wild ride through northern Ohio to Toledo. The FBI and Homeland Security were involved in reuniting John and Karen. In doing so, they learned that the six men were only a small part of a well-organized plan to cause the riot. The evidence trail led them back to the farm for a confrontation. During all of this, a budding romance was developing between John and Karen. Would it survive what was to come? Would law enforcement discover who was really behind the riot at the Capitol?

In 1961, Robert Lenhardt joined the military at age 17. He studied to become a Russian linguist for the Air Force Security Service. Upon finishing his service obligation in Berlin, Germany, he returned to civilian life where he entered private sector employment while he continued his education. In 1977 he formed his own contracting business. In 1983 he and his wife, Jean formed a manufacturing company, (Appleridge Stone), that grew into a business servicing and selling their product in eight states. The couple sold the business and retired in 2011. Stricken with myasthenia gravis in 2018, Robert was forced to give up most of his physical activities. When the Capitol riot occurred in January of 2021, Robert had the idea for this book. While it is a work of fiction, it is based on actual events. We may never know the complete story of what happened on January 6th, 2021.

Cast of Characters

Truman Mitchell "Mitch', leader of a group of rioters

    Robert Ball "Bolo", rioter

    Arnold Dinsmore "Dinny", rioter

    Ivan Kuznetzov "Tats" rioter

    Gregori Kravchenko "Bones", rioter

    Oleg Yermentov "Oreo", rioter

Donald Bevens "Secretary", conspirator

Unnamed "Chairman", conspirator

Wade Dilmore "Boss", leader of M-2 group (Detroit)

M-1, M-2, and M-3, unnamed conspirators

Karen Grant, nurse working in Florida.

Joyce and Robin, nurses working with Karen.

Martha Grant, Karen's widowed mother

Kurt Grant, Karen's brother

Sheila Grant, Kurt's wife

Bobby and Nancy Grant, Kurt's young children

Richard Fleming "Phlegm", Bolo's cousin (illegal gun dealer)

Jose' Cantina, Mount Pleasant policeman, friend of Grants.

Jubila Cantina, Jose's wife

John Osmond, former Green Beret

Tracy, John's friend at Ft. Jackson

Roger, John's ride from Ft. Jackson to the truck stop.

Judy, Roger's wife

Marie Wetsome, Lady who saves the day at turnpike rest area.

Willard Wetsome, Marie's husband

Todd Farley, Homeland Security Agent & helicopter pilot

Russ Quint, Homeland Security, flying 'second seat'.

Charles Stewell "Chick", FBI Agent

Connie Faye Palmori, "Connie", FBI Agent

Chief Tallman "Chief", Chief of Police in city of Toledo

Amy, hotel concierge in Toledo

Trooper Weaver, state police in Pennsylvania

Trooper Cooper, state police in Ohio

Trooper Maddie, state police in Ohio, partner of Trooper Cooper

Jimmy Sylvan, attorney for Wade Dilmore.

Nat McElhenny, private investigator for Jimmy Sylvan

Tim Patz, creator of the bolt head bug

Marge, Tim,s wife

Sergeant McLaughlin, Ohio State Police Barracks Chief

Pattycakes, the barracks dispatcher

Loretta and Heather, waitresses at Dean's Diner

Lieutenant Long, Commander of PA State Police Barracks

Jake the Bull

Dr. Nayar, Veterinarian for Jake

Daisy the Cow

And a cast of thousands at the U.S. Capitol

Made in the USA
Monee, IL
21 July 2021